Dear Reader,

Welcome home! Even if you've never been to Shelter
Valley before, you'll soon realize you've got a home
here. Anyone with a big heart is welcome in this
Arizona town, where folks look out for each other,
sometimes struggle with each other, always share each
other's pains and triumphs.

It's an especially exciting time here because Shelter
Valley's own prodigal son, Sam Montford IV, heir to
the town's founding family, is finally returning home
after ten years of silence. And he's not alone. He
has a seven-year-old daughter with him. His ex-wife,
whom he still loves and who still loves him, is single
and living in Shelter Valley again. Could be the
makings of a happily-ever-after...

What I hope will really make you feel at home is
the fact that all is not perfect in Shelter Valley. Just
like anywhere in the world. We all have faults. And
sometimes finding them in others is comforting, makes
them more like us, allowing us to relate to them more
easily. Sam Montford made a substantial mistake. But
he's ready to atone for that mistake and to share with
Shelter Valley the good things he's created in his life.
He asks only to be forgiven.

And in Shelter Valley he has a chance of finding that
forgiveness. This is the gift I wish for you—a true
home, a sheltering home. A home where love is
unconditional, acceptance a promise kept and
forgiveness a reality.

Sweet dreams,

Tara Taylor Quinn

Tara Taylor Quinn is a popular writer for
Harlequin's Superromance series; she is known for
her deeply emotional and psychologically astute novels.
Sheltered in His Arms is connected to her successful
Superromance trilogy, "Shelter Valley Stories" (but of
course can be read on its own).

Tara was first published in 1993 and has been a finalist
for the prestigious RITA Award. She lives in Arizona with
her husband and daughter. Besides being a full-time
writer, Tara is a board member of Romance Writers of
America.

You can reach Tara at P.O. Box 15065,
Scottsdale, Arizona 85267-5065 or online
at http://members.home.net.ttquinn.

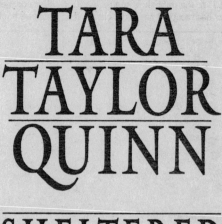

TARA TAYLOR QUINN

SHELTERED IN HIS ARMS

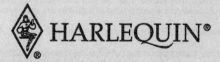

HARLEQUIN®

TORONTO • NEW YORK • LONDON
AMSTERDAM • PARIS • SYDNEY • HAMBURG
STOCKHOLM • ATHENS • TOKYO • MILAN • MADRID
PRAGUE • WARSAW • BUDAPEST • AUCKLAND

ISBN 0-373-83466-7

SHELTERED IN HIS ARMS

Shelter Valley is about friendships, the kind that go beyond the ordinary. It's about friends who become a family all their own. I lovingly dedicate this book to the three such friends I've been blessed with in my life:

Jeanine Lynn Clayton (1960-2000).
My childhoood soul mate. An integral part of my life that transcends the tragedy this temporal existence handed us. Your life was and always will be a part of me. With me. Sitting on my shoulder.

Kevin Scott Reames.
My partner, my champion, my lover.
You helped me find the me I was meant to become and loved the person who emerged.
Together, forever. That's me and you.

Patricia Anne Meredith.
My own private angel. You continue to teach me to believe in things that matter, to hope, to find good in the world around me. Just as you do. My eternal soul mate.

CHAPTER ONE

HER HIGH-HEELED evening sandals hadn't been made for sprinting across gravel. And the Montfords' desert landscaping was full of it. The darkness made things even worse.

But she had to get away—get out. She had to handle this news alone.

There was an old gnarled pepper tree in the corner of the yard and she hurried toward it. One branch had grown sideways, forming a natural bench with the other branches hanging down around it. Because of the balmy late-March weather they'd been enjoying in Shelter Valley, the tree was thickly covered with leaves. She could safely hide there.

For the moment. Until someone decided to turn on the outside lights.

"Ouch!" Cassie Tate's headlong rush from the house halted abruptly.

Damn!

She bent to pull a cactus needle from her shin. One quick jerk—a sting—and it was gone. When had her ex-in-laws gotten that cholla plant? It hadn't been there a few months ago, when she'd been over for a Christmas drink and gift exchange with them.

Unmindful of her new silk dress, Cassie slid onto the rough bark of the branch, its horizontal shape familiar to her. The first time Sam had ever kissed her had been right here...

Cassie looked around, her hands poised on the trunk as though she were ready to push off. Maybe it had been a mistake to come out here.

But where else could she go? The backyard was enclosed with an eight-foot-high stucco wall. She couldn't get out front—and to her car—without walking through the house.

Breathe, she reminded herself. She filled her lungs as much as her tight chest muscles would allow.

She had to be calm. To assimilate what she'd just heard. And what she was going to do about it.

One thing was for certain. She *wasn't* going to cry. She'd cried enough tears for Samuel Montford.

Glancing through the leaves surrounding her, toward the house where strains of piano music wafted from the living room, Cassie could see the lights of the party twinkling merrily. As though everything was normal.

And maybe for all those people in there, things were just fine.

Maybe all of *them* could welcome Sam home after his ten-year desertion. Maybe they could forgive. Forget.

Maybe she could, too. If she had a million years to try.

Sitting out here, on their tree, her mind wandered back to the boy she'd known and loved with all her heart. She thought of the passionate dreams he'd poured out to her beneath these branches. He'd wanted to save the world back in those days. Get rid of poverty, pain, injustice.

He'd promised to love her forever.

"Oh, God, Sam. Why?"

Her words sounded shockingly loud in the night. Cassie took a long, shuddering breath. How many times had she asked the same question over the past ten years?

"Can't you at least just leave me in peace?" she whispered, tears pooling in her eyes.

She used to dream of great things. Of love and family and children. Of happiness and warmth. Now all she hoped for was peace. It was the only option left.

"Cassie? You out here?"

It was Zack. Her partner. Her friend. He'd know how she was feeling. Without her saying a word, he'd know.

His footsteps were getting closer. Cassie pulled herself in, hardly daring to breathe as she waited for him to pass. She couldn't face him yet. Couldn't face anyone.

Not until she was sure she wouldn't fall apart. She'd done that once, back then, suffered a debilitating breakdown, and emotional collapse.

She'd done it after Sam had left her, after her baby girl had died, after she'd been told she'd probably never be able to conceive again.

But those dark days had helped her find the strength and awareness she needed. She'd gone on to finish college, to become a nationally renowned doctor of veterinary science. She was successful. She wasn't going to fall apart again just because her adulterous ex-husband had decided to return to town.

Though she couldn't help wondering why he was coming back. The way she remembered it, he hadn't been able to leave fast enough. And he hadn't been in touch with any of them since—other than infrequent calls to his parents to let them know he was okay. And to make certain that they were.

What had he been doing all these years? And with whom?

These were questions Cassie had tried so hard never to ask.

What had the years done to him? Another question she'd shied away from. But one that was apparently to be answered soon.

Were his eyes still that deep green? Did they still

have that penetrating directness? Her stomach tightened just thinking about them. About what a look from him used to do to her.

One time, she'd been looking for him in the highschool cafeteria. Her class right before lunch had gotten out late and she hadn't seen him in line. She'd gone through, anyway. Bought a salad and a soda, and was standing there with her tray, wondering what to do when she'd seen him come in through the door at the back of the room. He'd been frowning—until he saw her. And then his eyes had lighted with such familiar, knowing warmth that her belly had fluttered, her knees had fluttered—and she'd dropped her tray.

Sam had always been a looker. Was he still?

Was his dark hair still as soft as the finest silk, still as thick?

Did he have any of the wrinkles she'd been noticing around her own eyes lately? Had he gained any weight?

Sniffling, Cassie wiped the tears from her cheeks. God, she missed him.

Missed the boy she'd loved since she was twelve years old. The man she'd married—and lost—more than a decade ago.

She missed the dreams. And the dreaming.

"Damn you, Sam Montford," she whispered, sniffling again. "Damn you for what you did. And for coming back now…"

The man might return to Shelter Valley, but as far as Cassie was concerned, he'd lost the right to call this town home.

MARIAH WAS STILL ASLEEP. Sam's heart swelled with love—and worry—as he glanced over at the child on the reclining passenger seat beside him. He should have sold the truck, bought a car. Something she could get into without climbing up on hands and knees.

Something that felt more like it belonged to a family than a roaming man.

Mariah might not know it, might not believe him when he told her, but they were almost home. At last.

In all the years he'd lived in Shelter Valley, the place had never felt as much like home as it did now. This journey back was so important. So life-changing. So right.

And so damn scary.

But he was ready.

The little girl stirred, her skinny legs stiffening as she stretched. Their boniness, visible beneath her new denim shorts, scared him. She'd been wearing pants all winter, and her loss of weight hadn't been as noticeable. Or maybe he'd just been too afraid to acknowledge that she was wasting away.

He had to get her to eat more. To eat, period. He

wasn't going to let her die. He wasn't going to lose her, too.

"Good afternoon, sleepyhead," Sam said cheerfully, smiling at the little girl who'd stolen his heart in the delivery room seven years before. Her parents, his closest friends in the world, had insisted he be there with them. "How's my girl?"

Mariah looked at him.

That was all. Just looked. It was all she ever did anymore.

Heart heavy, Sam continued with cheerful chatter. Keep talking to her, the doctors had told him. Surround her with love. She'll never forget the tragedy, but she can recover.

He'd been talking for six months.

And Mariah had yet to say a word.

"You just wait until you meet your new grandparents," Sam told the child. "I was an only child, too, just like you. And my mom and dad were the greatest. You'll love them, but they'll love you more. Not that you need to let that worry you. That's just the way they are."

The landscape was painfully, blissfully familiar. Yet different.

"Mom makes the best chocolate chip cookies in the world." He glanced over again and decided to feel encouraged by the fact that Mariah was still watching him. Even if that was about all she ever did.

Maybe she was listening, too.

"Sometimes, when I was a kid, I'd sneak down from my bed at night, just to have another one of those cookies. I tried really hard to be as quiet as a mouse so I wouldn't get caught," Sam said. The smile he'd plastered on his face, became real as he remembered those days. "Every time a step creaked, my stomach would jump and I'd stand still and not breathe until I was sure my mom hadn't heard me."

Mariah blinked, her sad little face turned up toward his. Shelter Valley was going to be good for her. It had to be. If the answers weren't there, if the love in Shelter Valley wasn't enough to heal her, nothing would.

"The cookie jar was this big glass thing and the lid was really heavy and I'd have to lift it really carefully..."

The approaching sign said Shelter Valley, One Mile. The sign was new.

At least, it hadn't been there ten years ago.

Sam wiped his palm along his denim shorts.

"...the hardest part, though, was putting the lid back without making a noise. Especially because by that time I was always afraid I'd get caught and have to put the cookie back."

Sam slowed, approaching the exit. Mariah's gaze never left his face. She didn't look around, didn't show any interest at all in the place that was going to be home to her. He wondered how it was possible for someone with her naturally dark complexion to look so pale.

"I'd creep slowly back up the stairs, the smell of that cookie in my hand teasing me the whole way."

There was a new gas station at the Shelter Valley exit. And the huge old tree was still shading the east side of the road.

"It was sure a lot of work, but boy, when I finally made it back to my room and sank my teeth into that cookie, mmm." Sam grinned at Mariah. "It was worth it. Just for that one bite."

He passed the road that led out to the cactus jelly plant. The street sign still had those familiar BB gun dents put there by some guy who'd gone to high school with Sam's parents. No one had ever told Sam *which* guy, just "some guy."

A few scattered houses came into view, then disappeared as he drove past. He wondered what Mariah thought of them, as he tried to see Shelter Valley through her eyes. Through fresh eyes.

Not that she'd have any opinion of those houses. She wasn't seeing them. She was still staring at Sam.

"You want to know the funniest thing about my cookie escapades?" he asked, glancing over at her.

She blinked. A regular occurrence, but Sam chose to take this particular time as a yes.

"When I was in high school, my mom told me that she'd known all along I was stealing those cookies. She and my dad would sit in the family room and listen for me to come down the stairs…"

They'd smiled at each other, sharing their joy in their only son. She hadn't told Sam that, but he'd known. No parents had ever delighted in their child more than Sam's parents had.

Until the day he'd hurt them beyond belief.

"…all that work was for nothing." Sam finished his story as he slowed, entering the town proper.

Sunday afternoon had always been a sleepy time in Shelter Valley. It still was. Sam was relieved. He welcomed the comfort born of knowing this place. Craved its predictability.

Yearning for a drive through these remembered streets, for reassurance as he reacquainted himself with the place he'd always called home, for even a glimpse of the woman who still held such a place in his heart, Sam turned his truck and headed up the mountain, instead.

To the home he'd grown up in. He and Mariah had been driving for three days. His little girl needed to get those legs on solid ground—and since it had been two hours since their last stop, probably needed to go to the bathroom, too.

She didn't need a trip down her father's memory lane. Her father of only a few months…

"There it is, honey," he said, his throat tight as

the huge house became visible, off in the distance.
"See, it's just like I told you. A big beautiful castle
up on the mountain."

Montford Mansion. The place he'd loved and
hated with equal fervor.

Mariah had been staring at the insignia on his
glove compartment, but when Sam spoke, her eyes
turned toward him again.

"Look, Mariah, the orange trees are filled with
blossoms."

Damn, it felt good to be home, in spite of all the
resurrected pain the old sights were bringing him.
The regrets.

The knowledge that he was going to have to see
his Cassie with another man, married to another
man. After all this time, she would've found someone to love. Someone who wouldn't betray her faith
in him, her loyalty. She'd probably have several
kids by now. She'd wanted at least four.

Reaching out, he stroked a couple of fingers
lightly down Mariah's cheek. "You're the princess
of the castle now, remember, sweetie?" he said,
trying his damndest to help his daughter feel a little
magic again, to believe in the fairy tales that thrilled
most seven-year-old girls. He fingered one of the
waist-length black braids he'd painstakingly tied
when they were back in their hotel room in Albu-
querque this morning. "That's why we did the

braids, remember?'' he coaxed. ''So you can wear your crown like a real princess.''

He'd bought the crown more than a week ago, before they'd left Wilmington, Delaware. With its glittering glass jewels, it had cost him almost a hundred dollars—no plastic piece of junk for his little girl. He'd have paid ten times that amount if it would make Mariah smile again.

Slowing the truck, overwhelmed by unexpected emotion, Sam wound around the curves that would take him up the mountain to his parents' driveway. His driveway, really. He was the only living heir to Montford Mansion.

Not that any of it meant a whole lot to Sam. He was the fourth-generation descendant of Shelter Valley's founder, but his heritage had been far more of a burden to him than a blessing.

That burden wasn't going to stop him from coming home. Shelter Valley was Mariah's only hope.

And maybe Sam's, too.

THE HOUSE LOOKED exactly as he'd left it. Driving slowly, Sam approached the circular drive, heart pounding in spite of his admonitions to the contrary. This wasn't going to be easy. He knew that. He'd come fully prepared to accept the hostility that was his due. Prepared to make amends as far as was humanly possible for destroying the hopes and dreams of those who'd loved him so faithfully.

Parking in front of the house, Sam sat and stared, taking in the heavy double doors, the stucco walls, the shrubbery under the huge picture windows. As a little kid, he'd been paid a buck an hour to clean up behind the gardener who trimmed those shrubs.

A buck an hour. To a kid who was a millionaire in his own right. But what had *he* known? He'd wanted to grow up and be a gardener someday. To make some of the dingy houses in town look as beautiful as his did. Even then, working with his hands had been all Sam cared about.

Sam's finger itched now, for the drawing pencil that was never far away these days. His mind was reeling with stories for next week's strip.

Mariah's small brown hand slid across the seat and stole into Sam's. Turning, he met the frightened eyes of his little girl—and felt traces of the heartache that would never ease.

"You're going to love it here, honey. See all the pretty flowers your grandma has growing in the yard?"

Mariah continued to gaze at him, unblinking now, and suddenly Sam wasn't at all sure about what he was doing. Unbuckling Mariah's belt, he pulled her across the seat and onto his lap, cradling her protectively in his arms.

Shelter Valley was her only hope. He knew that. The people in this town, with their huge hearts and warm smiles, would coax his little girl out of the silent world of terror into which she'd sunk. They'd teach her to smile again. To play. They'd make her laugh. Forget.

Maybe, someday, she'd even find the courage to love.

He wondered if his parents still had Muffy, the cocker spaniel he and Cassie had bought them shortly after Sam had left home to marry Cassie. The dog would be almost twelve years old.

Best not get Mariah's hopes up on that one. Or Sam's, either. He'd been very partial to that dog.

"It's going to be okay, baby, it's going to be okay."

Mariah shuddered, her little hand coming to rest in his again. Sam could only imagine the thoughts running through the child's mind—terrifying images of the tragedy that had torn her life apart.

Looking at the familiar front door of the big house that had been both prison and haven to Sam, he wondered if maybe he should go back to Phoenix, get a hotel room, tuck Mariah in for a nap and call his parents from there.

He'd sent them a brief note, almost three weeks ago, telling them he'd be arriving some time soon.

A brief note. That and a few very short phone calls were all the communication he'd had with them in the ten years since he'd left home in disgrace. They knew nothing about his life since. Nothing about Mariah.

And he knew nothing about them, other than that they were both healthy. Nothing about the state of his father's business, the small but prestigious investment firm James had founded thirty years ago. He knew nothing about Shelter Valley, except for what he'd seen on the drive in. From the moment he'd walked out of his and Cassie's house that Saturday morning, his parents had never mentioned her again. And after he'd left town two weeks later, they'd never mentioned Shelter Valley, either.

He'd never even received divorce papers, although he'd signed documents before he left town, allowing Cassie to terminate their marriage. He'd never given anyone a forwarding address.

He'd never expected to come home.

He'd purposely kept the time of his arrival vague. Hadn't wanted them to be waiting for him, or to have anyone else waiting to welcome him home. Hadn't been able to bear the thought of their *not* waiting, either, if truth be known.

But for Mariah's sake, he'd needed to arrive in town with as little fuss as possible.

Now, sitting outside his childhood home, he felt like a fool. How could he take his fragile little girl in there, with no idea of what she'd have to face. Sam was all she had left in the world. How would she react if his parents were rude to him?

Or worse, indifferent? Cold?

A chill swept through him, in spite of the child

sweating against him and the Arizona sunshine
beating down on his truck. He had to turn around.
Go back to Phoenix. He couldn't risk creating any
more anxiety or tension in Mariah's life.

His parents were going to love her. He knew that.
But he also knew he had to smooth her way. Give
them a chance to speak their piece against him
without her witnessing it.

And maybe he needed a little more time than
he'd realized, as well—

"Sam?" The voice came from far off, but Sam's
heart recognized the call immediately. "Sam, is that
really you, son?"

His mother came running out of the big front
doors of Montford Mansion, almost tripped over her
own feet as she came around to his side of the truck.

"Yeah, Mom, it's me," he said under his breath,
before pulling open the door. Mariah's fingers dug
into him, and she buried her face against his shoulder, just as his mother threw her arms around his
neck and kissed him.

"Oh, son, let me look at you," she said, crying,
smiling, trembling all at once. "I've missed you so
mu—"

Her words broke off, and Sam, watching her
face, knew she'd seen Mariah. Her eyes filled with
wonder, with curiosity—and fresh tears—as she
pulled back.

Sam grabbed hold of her hand.

Taking a deep breath, offering a short silent prayer, he ran his other hand down his daughter's coal-black hair. "This is Mariah, Mom. I adopted her three months ago. She's been waiting to meet you."

CHAPTER TWO

"HEY! ZACK AND I are on our way to my folks' for a barbeque and swim. You want to come along?"

Cassie jumped, her pen slashing across the journal subscription form she'd been filling out. The voice coming from her office doorway—when she'd thought herself alone in the clinic—gave her a shock. Not her partner's voice, as she might have expected, but his wife's. Zack would have made a lot of noise as he entered, to warn her that she wasn't alone.

In case she'd been doing something private. Like crying…. Reaching for the remote just beyond her right hand, Cassie turned down the volume on the small television she'd been listening to while she worked.

"I've got reports to catch up on," she said, smiling in spite of her refusal. Zack Foster had been her sole confidante and best friend for more than nine years. They'd met after she'd left Shelter Valley to finish her education in Phoenix. Now that he'd married Randi, she had a second best friend.

A friend who was far less predictable than
Zack—

Randi leaned over Cassie's desk, peering at the
paperwork she'd just messed up. "Looks like important stuff to me," Randi said, raising both eyebrows.

Cassie pointed to the pile of manila folders
stacked in the tray on the far corner of her desk.
"Those are the reports."

"That pile doesn't look as big as Zack's."

And he has time to take the day off, Cassie finished for her.

"He writes faster than I do." She had no intention of crashing her friends' family gathering, but
Cassie didn't mind continuing their banter. Even
though she intended to stand by her refusal, she was
actually enjoying herself. She enjoyed arguing with
Randi over big issues and small ones. Randi's professional sport days might be over, but the woman
was a born competitor.

"Ah," she was saying now, "but it takes Zack
longer to figure out what to say."

"And I have to supply forms to fill out. My medical supply rep is coming by first thing in the morning. Your husband tends to get a little testy when
he doesn't have the syringes he needs."

Randi shoved aside the folders and perched on
the corner of Cassie's desk. "It's not good for you
to be here alone on a Sunday afternoon."

Though Randi's concern wasn't necessary, Cassie was warmed by it. "The last million or so haven't hurt me any."

"That's debatable."

"I'm fine, Randi, really," Cassie said, brushing a lock of red hair away from her face. She usually wore it pinned up or tied back, but since she'd been planning to spend the day alone, she hadn't bothered with her hair. Or her clothes, either. She was wearing jeans she'd owned since high school.

Randi frowned, apparently not satisfied with Cassie's assurances. But then, Randi was stubborn. It was hard for her to accept being wrong. It usually took her a couple of minutes to figure out that she was.

"How'd your meeting with Phyllis go yesterday?" Randi asked, referring to a mutual friend, psychiatrist Phyllis Langford.

"Wonderful," Cassie said. "Even better than I'd expected." Her enthusiasm for the pet therapy project she and Phyllis had discussed infused Cassie's voice. "She gave me some great insights that I'm going to incorporate into my next article. And an idea for a case I worked on back east this winter. A woman who'd lost several babies and was suffering from acute depression. Phyllis thinks a puppy might satisfy her mothering instinct to some extent, perhaps helping her accept adoption as another choice."

Randi scoffed, though Cassie knew full well that during the past months, working with Zack on his nursing-home project, Randi had been won over to the miracles that happened regularly through pet therapy. "You think a puppy who pees everywhere in the house, chews up her shoes and bites at her ankles is going to help the poor woman?"

"Brat's giving you problems, eh?" Cassie grinned. Zack had adopted the dalmatian puppy the week before, when the owner of its mother had despaired of finding the runt of the litter a home. Randi, though, had been the one to name him— Miserable Little Brat, or Brat for short.

"It's Zack's dog," Randi said, rubbing at the leather on her pristine white tennis shoe.

Cassie knew better. She'd been over at Randi and Zack's for pizza a few days earlier and had seen Montford University's seemingly tough women's athletic director cuddling that puppy.

Until Randi had noticed Zack and Cassie looking. Then she'd shooed him away, pretending to scold, while passing him a pepperoni slice under the table by way of apology.

"I don't know why he thought we needed another dog," she muttered. "As if Sammie and Bear aren't trouble enough."

Two of their trained pet therapy dogs, Sammie and Bear weren't any trouble at all. In fact, Zack had told Cassie that on a couple of occasions Randi had made excuses to take Sammie to work with her. Apparently, the dog was quickly becoming the mascot of the women's athletic department.

Cassie had Randi's number. The woman was strong when she needed to be and maintained an effective façade of toughness. But in reality, she was indeed the princess her family had always thought her. Tender, loving, frequently indulged. And kinder than anyone Cassie had ever known. With Zack's encouragement, she'd gotten over her lifelong fear of dogs, and a latent love of animals had begun to emerge.

Although she and Cassie had graduated from Shelter Valley High School the same year, had grown up together in Shelter Valley—population two thousand when the university wasn't in session—the two women had hardly known each other. Cassie had been completely besotted with her one true love, Samuel Montford the fourth, the town's esteemed future mayor and savior of the world. And Randi had been absent a lot of the time, training for her career in professional women's golf.

Neither woman's life had turned out the way she'd planned. They were both back in Shelter Valley, Cassie without Sam, and Randi with a bum rotator cuff that had ruined her swing.

"You'd better get back to your husband, or he's going to be in here looking for you," Cassie told her friend. Cassie knew her partner. Zack had all the patience in the world; he just didn't like to wait.

Randi shook her head. "No, he won't. He said you were going to be pissed if we kept hounding you, so he refused to come in. As a matter of fact, he went to get some gas and wash the Explorer."

Glancing at her watch, Cassie said, "Which means he should be pulling in right about now."

Randi didn't budge. "Other than the few times Zack and I've been able to coerce you over to our place, you've been hiding out in this clinic ever since you heard Sam was coming home," she said bluntly. "You can't keep hiding."

Retrieving another subscription form from a sample issue of the journal, Cassie started to fill it in. "I'm not hiding out. And I can do whatever I damn well please. That's the great thing about being single and living alone."

At least, she told herself that often enough. And it was true. Sort of. She *enjoyed* living alone. She had to. Or live her life without enjoyment.

"It's been three weeks," Randi said. "He's probably not coming back, after all."

"It doesn't matter to me one way or the other," Cassie lied.

"Uh-huh."

"Isn't your family going to be getting mighty hungry?" Cassie asked, still concentrating on the form in front of her.

"Dinner's not until five."

Oh. Great.

"Look," Cassie said, putting down her pen as she met her friend's gaze. "My life with Sam was a long time ago. I'm a different person now, and I'm sure he is, too."

"But that doesn't mean—"

"He killed any feelings I had for him when he went to another woman's bed," Cassie interrupted, before Randi could say anything she might have a hard time denying.

It was taking everything she had to keep her mind on the right track. And her heart from splintering into a million pieces with the force of bitterness and regret.

Randi stood up, headed for the door. "You need to learn how to lie better before you go trying it again," she said, getting the last word. "We'll bring some barbecue by your place later tonight. You'd better be there, or I'll make Zack come here and drag you out."

No question, Randi had won that round.

But Cassie would have her turn. She wasn't going to let anyone get the better of her again. Not her partner's new wife. And not the ex-husband she hadn't heard from in ten long years.

After three weeks of waiting, of constantly looking over her shoulder, of hiding out to avoid the chance of inadvertently running into Sam, Cassie's nerves were a little raw.

But maybe Randi was right. Maybe he wasn't coming, after all. His cryptic note had come three weeks ago. Surely it didn't take that long to get to Shelter Valley, no matter where he'd been.

It was time to get on with her life. She wouldn't give Sam the opportunity to rob her of it again.

Sam. Where had his letter come from, anyway? The postmark had been someplace back east. But the letter had been sitting on James Montford's desk for a day or two before his wife had happened upon it in the middle of a party—a celebration to welcome their long lost nephew into the fold. She'd gone to the library to check on her guests' sleeping babies, had come through James's office on her way back to the party, and had been reaching for a tissue on his desk, when she'd knocked a pile of unopened mail onto the floor.

She'd recognized her son's handwriting on the envelope with no return address. After ten years, she still recognized Sam's handwriting.

Cassie knew she'd have recognized it, too.

What else about Sam would be recognizable?

No. She shook her head, pulled the stack of files toward her. She wasn't going to spend another minute of her life thinking about something that hadn't been real for a very long time.

He wasn't coming, anyway.

THE CLINIC WAS NEW, built since he'd left town.
Not too far off Main Street, it sat on a lot that had
been vacant Sam's entire life. With its fresh stucco
finish and smoothly paved parking lot, the clinic
spoke of success.

It spoke of Cassie.

Leaving his truck parked under the shade of a
tree, Sam took Mariah's hand, drawing as much
comfort as he gave. Somehow, his having a child
made facing Cassie more tolerable. He didn't question that Cassie would have a family; it was all
she'd ever wanted. He wondered briefly about the
man she must have married—someone he knew?—
then dismissed the thought. It occurred to him that
in some ways, Mariah's presence put him and Cassie on a more equal footing. They'd both moved
on. She wouldn't be the only one who was a parent
now. They were both parents...although not of each
other's children. He slowly approached the door of
the veterinary clinic. It was Monday morning; he
wasn't ready for this. Could hardly drag the air
through his lungs. But he'd become a man who
faced hardships and challenges head-on, and this
was one of the biggest.

There were only a couple of cars in the parking
lot. He hoped one was Cassie's. And that she'd
have a minute or two to spare for him. While he
and his parents had spent a miraculous five hours

talking the night before—about their lives and his, about Mariah—they'd never mentioned Cassie.

The unspoken message was very clear.

He'd have to clean up this mess on his own. And until he did, his parents weren't going to give him anything where Cassie was concerned. They loved her like their own daughter. Always had.

They were on her side.

Sam couldn't blame them. He'd be on her side, too, if there were any way for a man to be in two places at once.

"We're going to see an old…friend of Daddy's," he told the silent child who'd refused to leave his side in the eighteen hours they'd been in town.

His mother had been enchanted—as Sam had known she would be—with Mariah. Though the little girl was completely unresponsive, at least outwardly, Carol Montford hadn't lost any opportunity to make contact. To touch Mariah's hand. To smile at her, tend to her, stroke her hair. To get some food—any food—into the child's stomach.

His father was already wrapped around Mariah's little finger.

Mariah just didn't know it yet.

She didn't know she'd met her match in those two. They were going to love Mariah back to life. Period. Between him and his parents, she wouldn't have a chance *not* to become the vivacious, happy child she'd once been.

They walked across the parking lot. "Her name is Cassie and she's just about the prettiest woman you've ever seen," Sam said, remembering.

He had to do this, to see her first thing. It wouldn't be fair to either of them to accidentally bump into each other in town. And he hoped that seeing her at work would mean he wouldn't be face to face with her children. Or her husband. At least not yet. Unless it was in the form of a photo on her desk.

It was what he wanted for her, what he'd been imagining all these years. A husband who deserved her love, who cherished her as Sam had promised *he* would. All the children she'd dreamed of raising. It was the only way he could live with himself, believing that without him she'd managed to have everything she wanted. That she was happy.

"She used to be Daddy's best friend, a long time ago."

Mariah walked solemnly beside him, her long black hair in a high ponytail tied with a blue bow that matched the jeans overalls and pink-flowered top he'd chosen for her that morning. Before the disaster that had changed her life so completely, Mariah had insisted on choosing her own outfits every day. And on doing her own hair, as well. She'd looked a little lopsided a time or two—but

Sam would trade that for the smile she'd worn any day.

She'd been so proud of herself back then. So sure that life was there just for her. Sure there wasn't anything she couldn't do, couldn't have, if she just got big enough.

She'd been sassy and confident and too smart for her own good.

And she'd chattered from the time she got up in the morning until she'd gone to bed at night, innocently sharing her every thought with anyone lucky enough to be around.

Sam had never tired of listening.

"Cassie is an animal doctor," Sam told Mariah now, as she hesitated outside the door of the clinic. "She's the one who gave Muffy to Grandma and Grandpa."

Muffy hadn't worked the magic on Mariah that Sam had hoped. The child, having always begged for a dog, had shown no pleasure at finding herself finally living with one.

But then, Muffy was old. And fat.

Sam had been saddened to see such obvious signs of the years he'd lost.

His parents had aged, too, but they still looked great. A little grayer, perhaps, a little more lined, but robust and healthy.

Apparently they walked a couple of miles every morning. And swam every afternoon. They were hoping to take Mariah out to the heated pool in the backyard with them this afternoon.

Sam wasn't sure he could persuade the little girl to let go of his hand long enough to walk into the next room, let alone outside the house. But he was willing to try. If anyone could reach Mariah, his mother could.

"Look, honey." He gently guided Mariah's head in the direction his finger was pointing. "See the plastic fire hydrant? That's for boy doggies to go to the bathroom."

Mariah might have been facing the fake hydrant, but he could see that she was still watching him out of the corner of her eye. Sam wished he knew what kind of expression could reassure the frightened child. A big smile? A calm, neutral look? A devil-may-care grin? He had no idea.

The inside of the clinic was as pristine and plush-looking as the outside. Brightly upholstered chairs lined the walls of the waiting room. At the moment, they were all empty.

There was a fancy digital four-foot scale along one wall. Sam supposed it was for animals. He liked the decor, the bright yellows and oranges, the tile floor that would serve for easy cleanup.

With Mariah by his side, Sam walked up to the waist-high solid oak receptionist's counter.

"Is Cassie in?" he asked, as though he stopped

by often. As though he wasn't asking a question he'd been yearning to ask for the past ten years.

"Dr. Tate?" the college-age girl asked. "Yes, she's in her office." She glanced down at the appointment book open in front of her. "Is she expecting you?"

"No," Sam said, glancing down at Mariah's head. "I grew up with her here in Shelter Valley. I'm an old friend, just dropping in to say hello."

"Oh!" The girl's expression changed from professionally polite to warm and friendly. "You're visiting?" she asked, rising to her feet.

Again, Sam glanced at Mariah. "Uh, no," he said. "I'm moving back to town. Just arrived yesterday afternoon."

"Welcome back, then," she said. "My name's Sheila." She grinned. "I've only been in Shelter Valley a couple of years, but I feel like it's been my town forever. I love it here."

The town had a way of doing that to people. Unless you were the "savior of the world," as Cassie had jokingly called Sam. The heir apparent, future mayor and all-around best guy for the job. The man loaded down with everyone else's expectations.

"Hi, Sheila. I'm Sam. You going to Montford?" he asked, years of Shelter Valley friendliness automatically kicking in.

The girl nodded. "I was, but I got married and

just recently had a baby. Now I work here full time.''

Mariah's little hand was getting sweaty inside his. Releasing it, Sam slid his arm around her shoulders, as he smiled at the receptionist. "She's in her office, you said?"

"Shall I tell her you're here?"

"No," Sam said quickly, and then added, "I'd like to surprise her, if you don't mind."

He didn't want to take the chance that Cassie would refuse to see him.

"Oh. Sure." Sheila grinned at him again. "You just go through that door, and down the hall. Her office is on the right."

"Thanks." Sam led Mariah through the open door. "Is her partner in?" he thought to ask as he passed Shelia. There had been two names on the placard out front.

"Zack?" the girl said. "Not yet. His first appointment today is at eleven."

Wondering if Zack was her husband as well as her partner, Sam braced his shoulders and strode forward. As a Peace Corps member and then a national disaster-relief volunteer, he'd spent the past ten years rescuing people from sickening, tragic situations.

He could handle a ten-minute meeting with his ex-wife.

CHAPTER THREE

NO MATTER HOW MANY TIMES Cassie flipped through the pages of her calendar, there were no upcoming trips written in anywhere. She'd traveled so much over the past eighteen months, launching her nationwide pet therapy program in cities and universities across the United States, that Zack had been left to handle much of their Shelter Valley veterinary practice by himself. Her travel schedule was why she'd invited Zack, who'd been working at a practice in Phoenix, to go into partnership with her in Shelter Valley. His first marriage had just ended, and he'd been eager for a new start. And now, two years later, Cassie's wedding present to him and Randi was to stay in town a while.

But damn, a trip sure would be nice. Help her put life in perspective again.

"Hey, stranger."

Planner pages between her fingers, Cassie froze, staring at the month of May. It was coming up in a matter of weeks. She'd be—

"Cassie?"

She hadn't imagined the voice. There was only

one man who said her name in just that way. With that slight emphasis on the second syllable.

Heart pounding, Cassie didn't know what to do. Sam was really back. After all this time.

She had to look up. To get through this. Making plans for May seemed so much safer.

Thank God, she was in her office. Private. No one was going to see if she messed up.

Except Sam.

He was standing in front of her desk. She could feel him there. She just couldn't bear to look at him. Couldn't be sure she wouldn't make a total idiot of herself and start to cry.

Sam hated it when she cried. Nearly as much as she did.

There was movement over there, close to Sam, but not really where he was standing. It drew Cassie's eye.

There, with her little hand clasped in a bigger one that could only belong to Cassie's ex-husband, stood a little girl. A very solemn, beautiful, dark-eyed little girl. She appeared to be part Native American.

"We—" Sam raised the child's hand "—Mariah and I just got into town last night. I couldn't be in Shelter Valley without seeing you first thing."

Oddly enough, Cassie understood that. She didn't like it, but she understood. She and Sam would never truly be strangers, or casual acquaintances who just had chance meetings on the street.

"You could have called first," she said, her eyes riveted on the child. His daughter? *His* daughter?

Pain knifed through Cassie, so sharp she couldn't breathe. When he'd left her all those years ago, he'd taken from her any hope that she might have children of her own. Taken away any hope of the family and the life she'd wanted. And now he had the nerve to waltz back into town with a child who should have been theirs.

"I was afraid you wouldn't see me," he murmured.

"You were probably right."

Was the child his? With her obvious coloring and that coal-black hair, the girl didn't look anything like him. Yet her white heritage was noticeable in those striking blue eyes.

Sam had green eyes.

"This is Mariah," Sam said, sounding less sure of himself as she continued to watch the silent little girl. "She's my daughter."

The knife sliced a second time. Lips trembling, Cassie nodded. And tried to smile at the child. After all, it wasn't Mariah's fault her father had hurt Cassie so badly.

"Hello, Mariah."

The little girl stared wordlessly at her father's waistline. Which, now that Cassie noticed it, looked as firm and solid as it always had. Clearly, Sam was still in remarkably good shape.

"You're looking great, Cass," Sam said, an old familiar warmth enlivening the words.

"Thanks." Taking a deep, shuddering breath, Cassie forced herself to look up, to meet Sam's gaze.

And then looked away again almost immediately. His eyes were exactly the same. They met hers—and touched her all the way inside.

Without waiting for an invitation, Sam sat in one of the leather chairs facing her desk, pulling Mariah onto his lap.

"How old is she?" she asked. Morbid curiosity.

"Seven."

Cassie's daughter would have been ten this year.

"So how've you been, Cass?" Sam asked, glancing around her office at the degrees on the wall behind her, the thick texts lining her shelves. "You've accomplished a lot."

Cassie stared at the little television in the corner. Wishing she hadn't turned it off after the news ended half an hour ago. It would have given her something to focus on. Taken her thoughts off the bitter pain that had already seized her.

Off the man in front of her.

"Your parents told you about the pet therapy program, I imagine," she said. It was the sum total of her life's accomplishments. Had they told him that, as well?

If this was just a guilt-induced duty call, he could leave now. She didn't need his polite compliments. Or his pity.

The flood of anger felt good.

"They haven't mentioned you at all," he said quietly. "I don't know the first thing about a pet therapy program. I'm just impressed with this office, the clinic, your degrees."

Cassie shrugged. "I imagine you went on to greater things. You're probably a lawyer by now."

Not that she cared. She just figured he'd finished college and pursued postgraduate work. Entered some highly regarded profession. Sam had been the more intelligent of the two of them. He hadn't particularly liked to hit the books, hadn't enjoyed learning as much as she had, but it had all come so naturally to him. Even in high school he could ace a test with a five-minute look over his notes, while Cassie would study for an entire evening to get the same grade.

"I don't even have a bachelor's degree."

Shocked, Cassie frowned at him. His hair was longer, his face lined with experiences she knew nothing about. "Why not?"

"I never went back to school after I left here." There was no apology in the words. No excuse, either.

"But you had a perfect grade point, a future..."

"...that I didn't want," Sam finished for her, his jaw firm. Then he smiled, which instantly softened his face. It was as though he'd learned to control the emotions that had once flowed so freely.

When they were young, Sam had been the most passionate man she'd known. Passionate about everything, from kissing her to saving an abandoned dog on the outskirts of town. She'd loved that about him.

"So what's this pet therapy business?" he asked. "Analyzing neurotic poodles?" He grinned in an obvious attempt to lighten the atmosphere, but his expression sobered when she didn't respond. "Seriously," he muttered. "Tell me."

Mariah's arm slid up around Sam's neck, and she lay her head against his chest.

She was too skinny. And quieter than any child Cassie had ever seen. It almost seemed as though something was wrong with her. Her stomach seized at the thought. The little girl was so beautiful.

She couldn't imagine Sam with a handicapped child. Everything had always come easy to him. Perfection had been his for the taking.

"I, uh, developed a bit of a name for myself by using animals as a way to treat mentally, and sometimes physically, ill patients," she said slowly, her attention on Sam's little girl.

There was something heart-wrenching about her.

Something pathetic in seeing her tucked so securely in Sam's arms.

Sam. She couldn't believe he was here. Sitting in her office. *Damn him.*

Her life wasn't ever going to be the same again, with Sam back in town. The memories, the reminders—they'd all be right in front of her. Mocking her. He'd just shot her carefully won peace all to hell.

Sam asked a few more questions—intelligent, thoughtful questions—about pet therapy, which Cassie managed to answer. Somehow, with him sitting there, work wasn't the first thing on her mind. It was an odd sensation.

A very unwelcome one.

SAM DIDN'T KNOW what he'd been expecting to find that morning, but the woman sitting across from him wasn't it. Her beauty was still as potent, her figure perfect, her hair still that glorious red. But despite all the similarities, he could hardly believe how much ten years had changed her. Was it just growing up that had made her so self-composed? So unemotional?

Or was it only with him that she was this way?

The thought sickened him. Saddened him. He'd carried the image of his vivacious and tender ex-wife with him every day of the past ten years, used

it as a sword to punish himself—and as a reminder
of the penance he owed.

"So who'd you end up marrying?" he asked
now, forcing himself to confront reality, to see the
woman Cassie had become, to not linger on memories of the days when he'd known her as well as
she'd known herself. "You are married, right?"

Cassie shook her head, and Sam froze.

"You aren't married?" he asked, his shock more
evident than he would have liked. She *had* to be
married. It was all Cassie had ever wanted. Marriage and a family.

"There are a lot of successful single women
these days," she said, her tone tinged with sharpness. "I would never have been able to accomplish
everything I have if I was married. I've spent the
past couple of years traveling all over the country,
setting up pet therapy programs in universities and
in hundreds of mental-health facilities."

Sam stared at her, not understanding. "But you
wanted to be a wife and mother more than anything
in the world," he said.

He hadn't been wrong about that. Had he?

Cassie's gaze slid away from him, her shoulders
stiffening. "People change, Sam."

Mariah's fingers dug into Sam's neck; he rubbed
her back reassuringly.

"You never had children?" He just couldn't take
it in. Didn't want to. Didn't want to believe he'd

had anything to do with her decision. It was one of the reasons he'd left town and never come back. So that Cassie could get on with her life.

Or that was what he'd always told himself. He'd assumed, without question, that she'd meet someone, marry, have kids. He thought briefly of his syndicated comic strip—another secret. The origins of the Borough Bantam were unknown to the people of Shelter Valley and yet it was based on them. Cassie was the gazelle. And in one of last month's episodes, the gazelle had given birth to twins.

"I don't have any children," she said, then stood as though dismissing him. "I'm happy your parents finally have you back, Sam," she said, then added, "You always were the light of their life."

Another too-familiar stab of guilt hit its mark. Sam also stood, sliding Mariah down to the floor beside him. The child's eyes were pleading when he looked down at her. She was ready to go. Now.

Odd. He hadn't realized that he was learning to communicate with her, to understand her, even without words. The thought brought a strange sort of comfort.

"I guess I'll be seeing you around," he said, guiding Mariah back into the hallway. He needed to tell Cassie about Mariah. And he would, as soon as he had a chance to talk to her alone. He needed to tell her the child wasn't his. Or not biologically, in any case.

Cassie had never married. God, he felt sick. And ashamed. A bone-deep shame.

"Okay" was all she said. So why did he hear, *Not if I can help it?*

After ten years, she still hated him so much. He deserved it; he knew that. Why had he been foolish enough to hope that the years might have dulled the consequences of his sins?

Mariah walked stoically beside him down the hall, which seemed to have grown a mile longer during his stay in Cassie's office, and he realized that if he was going to get through this, he had to concentrate solely on his new daughter—her needs, not his own. Just as they reached the door that would lead them back to the waiting room, she turned, looking over her shoulder.

"Cassie's a nice lady, don't you think?" he asked gently, his heart rate speeding up.

Mariah didn't answer him, but for the first time since her parents were killed, she'd shown an interest in something. It might not be much, but it was a start.

At that moment, Sam was willing to settle for anything.

"Let's go see if Grandma has lunch ready, okay?" he asked, squeezing Mariah's hand.

He might as well have been talking to himself.

CASSIE DIDN'T SEE Sam again for two days. She was walking home from the clinic on Wednesday evening—since she'd left her car at home that morning—enjoying the balmy Arizona spring day, trying to work up some enthusiasm for the cabbage rolls she'd made over the weekend and was going to have for dinner.

She'd had a good day. Had helped a collie through a difficult birth, managing to save all six puppies and the mother, as well. They'd been so adorable, she hadn't been able to resist when the collie's owner had offered Cassie pick of the litter. Now that she wasn't going to be traveling so much, she'd been planning to get a dog. And she'd always loved collies.

"Can we give you a ride home?"

Still reacting to that familiar voice, even after all these years, Cassie didn't stop walking. "No, thanks," she called, barely glancing Sam's way.

He drove a white truck.

She'd have expected him to drive a Lincoln Continental, or some other expensive car. But the truck seemed to suit him. Not that she really knew anything about Sam, or what would suit him. Nor did she want to.

Back to cabbage rolls. Yes, they'd be good. She'd treat herself to two. That would leave two more meals' worth in the freezer. It was a good thing they'd only take a few minutes to microwave. She was getting hungry and—

"I have a cousin."

Sam came up behind her, on foot, Mariah's bony little legs moving quickly beside him. Glancing back, Cassie saw his truck parked at the curb.

What did he want with her, for God's sake?

"I know you do," she said aloud. She realized that the news had to be a shock. When he'd left, he was the sole Montford descendant, the family's one hope. Now he'd come home to discover that an unknown cousin had shown up.

"You've met him?"

"Yes."

Mariah's hair was braided today. Cassie could just picture Carol fussing over the little girl. Her ex-mother-in-law must be about the happiest woman in Shelter Valley these days.

Cassie was genuinely thrilled for Carol. She'd always loved the woman like a second mother.

Her own mother didn't even know Sam was in town. Her parents had left at the end of March for the six-month cruise around the world that they'd been saving half their lives to take. Cassie was glad they were gone. She had no idea how they'd react to Sam's reappearance. Her father, who'd had four daughters and no sons, had taken Sam's defection personally.

He'd also been the one who had to tell Cassie that her baby girl had died.

"What's he like?" Sam asked, slowing his pace now that he was even with her. Mariah walked between them, staring ahead, it seemed, at nothing. "Ben, I mean. My cousin."

Watching the child, Cassie frowned. "He's very nice," she said, wondering what was wrong with Sam's daughter. Wondering how to ask. "He came to town last fall, fell in love with his English teacher—who wasn't really a teacher at all, it turned out." She gave a quick shrug. "It's a long story. They're married now."

"Mom said he's got a daughter Mariah's age."

Cassie nodded, wishing her house wasn't still two streets away. She couldn't do this. Walk casually with Sam and the child who'd never be hers, pretending they could be friends. "She's not actually his, biologically. Did your mom tell you that?"

"Yeah." Sam nodded, his free hand in the pocket of his jean-shorts. His long legs were more muscled than she remembered. "She said he married a girl his senior year in high school who claimed he was the father of her child."

"She let him support her for almost eight years before she told him Alex belonged to her boyfriend, who was in prison."

"Mom said that Ben's being awarded full and permanent custody of her, though."

"Her real father beat—" Glancing down at the head bobbing between them, Cassie broke off. "He wasn't a very good father."

"I gather Ben is."

"Obviously you haven't met him yet," Cassie said, "or you'd *know* he was."

Sam nodded again. "You're right, I haven't met him, but Mom's pushing for a get-together."

"Ben's a great guy. Looks a bit like you." In fact he resembled Sam enough that Cassie had had a hard time liking the man when she'd first met him. But he was Zack's closest friend. Nowadays Cassie not only liked and respected him, she admired the hell out of him. Ben Sanders was a real man in the true sense of the word.

Too bad Sam didn't share those particular genes.... Cassie stopped her reaction even as it took shape. She wasn't going to do this. She wasn't going to grow old and hard with bitterness, entertaining nasty thoughts. She was okay now. Happy with her life. Surrounded by friends and family who loved her.

"Just seems odd, after a lifetime of being the only Montford heir, to find out that I'm not."

"It's not like your inheritance meant a whole lot to you the past ten years." Damn her tongue. She turned the corner, Sam and Mariah staying in step beside her.

"It doesn't mean squat to me."

He'd certainly said so with great frequency. But until he'd left, turning his back on the money, the position, the town, she'd never really thought he believed it. She'd always thought the complaints were just a habit left over from when he was a kid, railing against expectations.

Everyone did that. Complained about what their parents expected of them. It was a normal part of growing up.

"Then what's the problem with sharing it?" she asked him now, thinking how little Sam appeared to need the Montford fortune, and how much Ben and his new family did.

"He can have it all," Sam said without bitterness, as though he still meant the words completely. "It just feels odd to have been one thing your entire life, only to find that it's not what you are at all."

Cassie nodded, glancing down as Mariah's arm brushed against her leg. The child, moving silently between them, didn't seem to notice.

Relieved when they reached her block, Cassie firmly turned her thoughts once again to cabbage rolls. They'd smelled so good when they were baking on Saturday night.

"This is it," she said, stopping at the bottom of her driveway. If he expected her to ask him in, he was mistaken.

Sam hesitated, looking at the house she'd bought a few years before, in one of the more affluent neighborhoods in Shelter Valley.

"Nice place."

"I like it."

"It's big."

"Yeah." She did most of her pet therapy work from an office here at home. And used the rest of the rooms to indulge her amateur interest in interior decorating.

Cassie was beginning to think Sam's daughter couldn't hear. The child didn't even turn toward the house they were discussing. Cassie had heard the adage about children being seen and not heard, but this was too much.

Besides, she'd never figured Sam for that kind of parent.

A familiar pain tore through her at the thought of Sam as a father. She had to stay away from this man, dammit! He could destroy every bit of her hard-won composure, and his very presence threatened the contentment she'd so carefully pieced together.

The child, however, shouldn't suffer for her father's sins. Her silence tugged at Cassie. Bending down, face level with the striking little girl, Cassie smiled. "It was nice to see you again, Mariah."

Mariah didn't respond. And Sam gave no explanation. Surely if the child was deaf, Sam would have said. And how could she ask, in case the little girl *could* hear and know they were talking about her?

"Have you had any of your grandma's cookies yet?" she tried again.

Neither a nod nor a shake of the head. Mariah's

gaze seemed intent on the T-shirt tucked into Sam's shorts. Her fingers were clutching it. Hard.

Meeting Cassie's questioning gaze, Sam just shook his head.

"Well, if you haven't, you've got a treat in store," Cassie continued, simply because she didn't know what else to do. "They're the best."

"I told her."

Of course. He would have. He'd grown up with them.

They both had.

"Well, good night," Cassie said awkwardly.

"'Night."

She didn't look back as she walked to her door, let herself in and locked it behind her.

But she knew Sam stood there watching her.

CHAPTER FOUR

MARIAH DIDN'T WANT to go back to that house. Sam was driving up the hill, so she knew they were going back there. She didn't want to. She didn't belong there.

Sam's house was for happy kids who didn't know bad stuff. And grandmas were for happy kids, too. Mariah wasn't like that anymore. She'd cried, made too much noise when the bad men came. That was why they'd killed her mommy.

Sam's mouth was all tight, except when he seemed to remember that Mariah was looking at him. Then he smiled a good Sam smile.

She used to think Sam's smiles made her feel happy. Now she didn't care whether he smiled or not. Smiles couldn't really do anything. They couldn't stop bad stuff. They couldn't save you from the horrible men.

Sam didn't have to smile. He just had to stay breathing. Mostly that was what she watched. To make sure he was always breathing.

Mommy had been still holding Mariah's hand but she hadn't been breathing—and the men had made

Mariah let go of her. That was when they said Mommy wasn't coming back. But Mommy hadn't gone anywhere, she'd been right there with Mariah the whole time—so how could she come back, anyway?

Daddy had gone away with them after they hit him so many times and made his face bleed. When Mariah cried out for him, they yelled back at her and told her to shut up. If she made a sound, they were going to hurt Mommy. They said Daddy wasn't ever coming back, either. Sam said he'd stopped breathing, too. She hadn't known that about breathing before.

Daddy was put into a hole in the ground—

"You hungry, honey?"

Sam smiled at her now. Mariah didn't get hungry anymore. She just got tired from watching Sam's breathing.

Breathing stopped, and then some men shoved you into a hole in the ground. But first, sometimes, they cut you and made you bleed so much that a Band-Aid didn't work.

They scared you and did other things Mariah couldn't think about.

So she just thought about breathing. If she stopped breathing, they'd shove her in a hole, too.

SAM'S PENCIL SLID EASILY around the page, making a mark here, another there, until the familiar figures began to take shape. After so many years of drawing this cartoon strip, he was seeing it differently tonight. He was on overload with the past four days of memory and stimulation.

Borough Bantam. Sam's imaginary world was filled with non-human life, of the animal variety, mostly—each creature representative to Sam of the people he'd known all his life in Shelter Valley. There was the king—a grizzly bear—his father. His mother, the queen, a gentle brown bear. Will Parsons was a lion. His wife, Becca, Sam's readers knew as a book-reading lioness. There was Nancy Garland, a girl they'd known in high school; she was a gopher. Sam's parents had told him she was still in town, hostessing at the Valley Diner. Jim Weber, owner of Weber's Department Store, was a penguin. Hank Harmon was the big friendly skunk everyone in the Borough loved, in spite of his smell. Chuck Taylor was a leopard. And on and on...

Cassie was the gazelle. Graceful. Lovely. And unattainable.

He still hadn't found a moment away from Mariah—a chance to see Cassie alone. Although the more he thought about the whole damn mess, the more he wondered whether it would make a difference to her whether or not Mariah was his biological daughter. She was still his daughter. He had a child to raise, while Cassie did not.

And yet he couldn't understand why Cassie had made that choice—to remain unmarried and childless. Nor could he stomach the irrational fear that he was at least partially to blame.

Mariah was finally asleep; Sam had put her in the bed across from the desk at which he sat. His parents had given him a guest suite, as it had two beds and plenty of room for him and Mariah.

Sam hoped that it wouldn't be too long before Mariah hankered after the princess room down the hall. Its lacy white canopy, yellow walls, and pictures of tea parties were enough to tempt any little girl. Weren't they? As a teenager, Cassie had always loved his mother's fanciful guest room. The couple of times her family had been out of town and she'd stayed with them, she'd chosen that room. It had been updated since he left town—with new paint, different pictures, some fancy ladies' hats on a rack—but his impression was the same. He still felt like a clumsy oaf in ten-pound mountain boots whenever he walked in the door.

Characters appeared on the page in front of Sam, seemingly of their own accord. The pencil moved swiftly, filling in thought bubbles almost faster then he could think them....

The castle was in chaos. There was a stranger in their midst, a wild stallion. He claimed to know them. The king and queen had offered their usual warm-hearted welcome. Always trusting. Seeing good in the visitor although his heart might harbor unclean things.

The half-witted magistrate, so full of his own importance, didn't know that Borough Bantam had been invaded yet. Sam grinned as the rotund little worm slithered around his circle, certain that he was circling the world. That he controlled the entire globe. His bubble was easiest of all to fill. *I am. I am. I am.*

It was rumored that the newcomer—the stallion—posed a threat to the magistrate. The worm—Sam's version of Shelter Valley's mayor, Junior Smith.

Ten years older than Sam, Junior had just become mayor when Sam's father retired. That was the year before Sam left town. James Montford had suffered a bout of Crohn's Disease and needed to lower his stress level; as a result he'd stepped down from the mayoralty. That was when Sam really started to feel the pressure to run for mayor. The fact that he would win was a foregone conclusion. The office of mayor was of course an elected position, but politics in Shelter Valley had more to do with tradition than democracy. The town's mayor had almost always been a Montford—although, occasionally, a member of the less-reputable Smith branch of the family held office.

The newcomer sat off by himself, watching the confusion, detached. He couldn't care less about the worm. He was waiting. Though he didn't know for what. The plan would be made known to him in due time. He just had to be patient.

Sighing, Sam scribbled the finishing touch, the signature of Bantam's creator, *S.N.C.*, and dropped his pencil. Then he tore off the piece of drawing paper, folding it carefully and sealing it in an envelope for mailing in the morning—on time to meet his deadline. He methodically put all evidence of the work he'd been doing in the battered satchel, which he placed back on the closet shelf. Patience was the lesson of the week—for the comic strip's new character *and* for him.

Sam needed to find a truckload of it somewhere.

ON THURSDAY NIGHT, Cassie was getting ready for bed with the eleven o'clock news playing in the background—from the console television in her bedroom, the little portable in her luxurious ensuite bathroom and the nineteen-inch set out in her kitchen—when the doorbell rang.

Assuming the caller was a patient with an emergency, she quickly spit out her toothpaste, wiped her mouth and pulled a pair of jeans on over her nightgown. Grabbing from the hamper the black, short-sleeved cotton shirt she'd worn to work that day, she drew it over her head while she made her way to the front of the house. It never occurred to her to be alarmed, to think anything dangerous might be waiting on her porch. This was Shelter Valley. A lot of people didn't even lock their doors at night.

She opened the door, and when she saw who was standing there with his hands in the pockets of his jeans, her heart started to pound so hard she actually felt sick.

"Why are you here?" she asked. It was too late to go back, to return to the lives they'd once lived. And for her and Sam, there was no going forward.

He shrugged, the dark strands of his hair almost touching the shoulders of his white shirt. His eyes glistened beneath the porch light. "I'm a little lost here, Cass," he said, giving her a glimpse of the past—a glimpse of who they used to be. Two people who told each other everything.

She couldn't do that anymore, could no longer be that person. Her hold on happiness was too fragile. Too tenuous.

"Perhaps you should go back where you came from, then," she said, trying not to cry as she rejected the intimacy he was offering.

"I belong here."

"Since when?"

He looked down at his tennis shoes and then back up at her. "Can I come in?" he asked softly.

"No!" There was nothing for them. No point. She'd built a life for herself inside this house—a house in which there was not one bit of evidence that Sam Montford had ever existed.

"Please, Cass," he said, his eyes begging her. "You know if we keep standing out here, everyone'll have us married again by morning."

"Which is why you need to leave. Now."

"I can't."

"Sure you can."

"I find myself needing a friend tonight, Cass. And you're the best friend I ever had in this town."

Why tonight in particular? Why did he need a friend now?

"Then why don't you go back where you and Mariah came from? You obviously have friends there." God, she hated what he was doing to her. How she was acting around him. But if she didn't get defensive, she'd crumble into little pieces at his feet.

She'd needed him so badly for so many years. And had broken down when she'd lost him. She'd learned that *breakdown* was not an exaggerated or metaphorical description. It was exactly what had happened. And it had taken a lot of years to rebuild herself, to repair all the damage. She just couldn't afford to allow Sam Montford to enter her life again.

"There's nobody back there. I'm all Mariah's got. Her family was killed six months ago," he said, and then rushed on as though he knew his time with her was limited. "Mariah saw the whole thing, Cassie, and I'm losing her."

Sagging against the big oak door, Cassie slowly pulled it back, gesturing Sam inside.

Not for him. Never again for him. But for that sweet child with the haunted eyes.

"Where is she now?" Cassie asked, leading Sam from the homey comfort of her living room in to the library she'd decorated with impeccable formality and never used. She took one of the leather chairs; Sam slouched down in the other.

"She's asleep," Sam said. "Thankfully, once I get her to give in and go to sleep, she usually stays that way. She used to have a lot of nightmares, but they've decreased in the past month or so. My mother's sitting with her."

Cassie sat forward, already preparing to kick him out. "Carol knows you're here?"

"No." He shook his head. "I told her I was going out for some air. She encouraged me to take an hour or two for myself." That sounded like Carol Montford. Tending to her family made her happy. And she'd had so few opportunities in the past ten years. There'd only been her husband, James, who needed little—and Cassie.

Sam grinned suddenly, shocking her with the intensity of the effect that smile had on her. "She warned me not to drink and drive."

In the grip of remembered companionship, Cassie said, "As if you ever would." Sam had always been responsible about stuff like that.

About everything.

Except fidelity.

"Is Mariah deaf?" she blurted out, nervous, needing to get him out of her house.

Eyes clouded, Sam shook his head. "No." And then, looking around, said, "You don't have a dog?"

Cassie's toes were cold. She pulled her feet up on the chair, covered them with her hands.

"I've been traveling more than I've been home during the past couple of years," she said. "It wouldn't have been fair to have a pet and then desert it so often, but I did recently acquire a collie puppy. I'm waiting for her to be weaned from her mother before I bring her home."

Why did it matter that he know this? That he not think her lacking—cold and immune to the animals she'd dedicated her life to assisting?

"I can't believe how fat Muffy is."

"You need to convince your parents to put her on a diet, Sam. She almost died a few months ago."

They shared a concerned look. Muffy was special to both of them. They'd picked her out together as a comfort to Sam's mother, who'd been so sad after Sam moved out.

"Her food was cut in half as of yesterday."

That reminded her of Sam, the old Sam. See a need, take charge, make it better.

Or at least try....

"Why doesn't Mariah speak?" she asked, focusing somewhere just to the right of his chin. There could be no more meeting of the eyes. Sam's looks touched her in ways she could no longer welcome. "Does she talk to you? Is it just strangers she's so shy with?"

Frowning, Sam lifted his hands, then let them drop back to his knees. "She hasn't said a word in six months. To me or anyone."

"You said her family died. What happened? A car accident?" The tragedy sure explained some of the sadness she saw in Sam's eyes. The sadness reached out to her in ways she wanted to resist.

"They didn't just die—they were murdered by a band of terrorist thugs hijacking the airplane Moira and her husband, Brian, and Mariah were on." He shook his head. "They were the only family Mariah had, and my closest friends."

Cassie swallowed, her throat suddenly dry. *Mariah's mother had a husband.* "Where were they?"

"It was a small jumper plane leaving Afghanistan. The Glorys were the only Americans on board. The terrorists were part of an extremist group fighting for recognition."

Cassie remembered with horror the reports she'd seen on the news. "Out of forty people on the plane, only ten survived," she continued slowly, her heart heavy as she watched the despair on Sam's face. "Six women, three men—and an American child..." Her voice trailed off. Mariah. "At least those terrorists were caught," she said, the thought bringing little comfort.

Sam clenched his jaw, and his hands tightened into fists. "It was all over the news—another terrorist incident. Mom and Dad heard about it in Germany, but they had no idea, of course, that the tragedy had anything to do with me."

"You weren't with them?"

Sam shook his head, eyes dulled and faraway. Cassie had all but forgotten that she wasn't going to look into his face anymore.

"I was in New Jersey. I'd been there a couple of years, working with a guy who's restoring old houses. I came home from work one day to a call from an attorney in Delaware—which is where the Glorys lived when they weren't on assignment somewhere in the Third World. Their will named me Mariah's legal guardian."

"You didn't know that?" Cassie was confused. Apparently, he hadn't been able to make a go of marriage with this Moira, either. It must have complicated things when she'd married his good friend—not that Cassie wanted to hear anything about that. But wouldn't he, as Mariah's natural father, *expect* to have custody of her in the event her mother could no longer care for the child?

Sam nodded. "I knew," he said hoarsely. "I just didn't think there'd ever be a need...."

His voice broke off, and he lowered his chin as though holding back deep emotion. He'd loved the woman so much?

Another stab of pain left Cassie feeling weak and tired.

"When I got to Afghanistan to collect Mariah, she was this silent huddle with big frightened eyes." He paused. "Immediately after the funeral, I moved into the Glorys' home and began adoption proceedings. I tried to make her life as normal as possible, surrounding her with familiar things, but she hasn't responded very much. She's been in counseling since the beginning, but there's only so much medical science can do. She's suffering emotional pain, not some kind of chemical imbalance they can medicate. There is no diagnosis of a disease. There are always medications, of course, but some things you have to come out of naturally, on your own. Mariah has to *want* to return to us."

"So she hasn't spoken at all?"

"Not a word."

"Not even when she saw you?"

Sam shook his head.

"It's obvious she adores you."

"We've always been close," Sam said softly, almost apologetically, as his eyes met Cassie's. "Without you, she was my only shot at having a child in my life."

Cassie ignored the first part of that statement. "You and her mother split before she was born?"

"Her mother and I were never together," he said, his expression gentle. "At least, not in any child-making sense. Mariah's not my biological daughter, Cass."

The breath slowly left Cassie's lungs. She felt dizzy, light-headed. But not relieved. Whether or not Sam had had sex with Mariah's mother made no difference to her; he'd certainly had sex with other women.

At least one while he and Cassie were married.

Because she didn't know what else to do, Cassie sat and listened while Sam told her about his best friends, the Glorys. All three of them—Brian, who was full-blooded Chippewa, Moira, a Peace Corps brat, and Sam—had met when they'd been leaving for a two-year stint overseas as Peace Corps volunteers.

Mariah's name came from a song she'd always loved. It referred to the wind. Sam said Mariah blew into their lives unexpectedly, but that she was vital to the very air they breathed.

While Cassie had been mourning their lost child, fighting to recover her life, Sam had been overseas making friends and helping other people, instead of caring for the wife he'd promised to love, honor and cherish. He'd been taking part in raising another child.

She'd have to tell him about that someday. When she was ready. When she felt she could get through the telling without falling apart. Emily's premature birth—and subsequent death a month later—wasn't something she spoke about. Ever. Even after all this time, the wounds were too raw. And it wasn't as though she owed Sam an explanation. He'd lost all rights to Emily when he'd deserted them.

Although she knew Sam wasn't responsible for the death of their child, any more than she was, she couldn't stop believing that if only he'd been there...

Yet, no matter how frozen her heart felt at this moment, Cassie was still glad to hear that he'd been doing something worthwhile during those years. Glad to know that, while he hadn't been there for his own child, little Mariah had been able to count on him.

Cassie had always figured he'd been enjoying the beds of coeds, like the girl he'd been with the night he should have been home with Cassie. Despite everything, she felt somehow consoled that this wasn't the case.

"We were pretty much the only family any of us had," Sam said, obviously lost in time. Cassie hated the stab of jealousy she felt as she heard the affection in Sam's voice for these unknown people.

She'd never been petty. Or possessive. She sure as hell wasn't going to start now. Sam was nothing to her. Less than nothing.

He'd betrayed her trust. Nothing was going to change that. Ever.

She might someday be able to forgive him. Had been aiming toward that goal for the past several years. But even if the day came when she could be truly free of the pain he'd caused her, the trust was gone. Once trust was broken, it couldn't be restored. It simply ceased to exist. How could you believe in someone you couldn't believe?

"Moira's parents were still alive back then, though they're both gone now." He shook his head grimly. "I'm glad they weren't around to know what happened to their daughter. They died of a viral infection in Africa, within a week of each other. Even when they were alive, they were always in service somewhere obscure. She saw them once a year if she was lucky. And Brian was an orphan."

Sam didn't bother to explain about his own aloneness. Perhaps there wasn't any point.

He gave a sudden laugh, and Cassie sensed sadness there as well as mirth. "I was the one who proposed," he said.

"To Moira, you mean?" So he and Brian had both been in love with the woman?

"No." He steepled his fingers in front of his chest. "They were such blind fools. Even after they were expecting Mariah, they couldn't figure out that they were crazy about each other. I had to point out the obvious and then drag them off to Atlantic City to tie the knot before they could talk themselves out of it."

Cassie had never had a friendship that close. Not since Sam. She envied him.

She had Zack, though. And Randi now, too. Zack had pulled her through some rough times in those first days after she'd made the decision to get on with her life and reenter college. At Arizona State, not Montford University. There was no way she could have gone back to Montford.

"When Mariah was born, I had to do most of the coaching because poor Brian was so scared seeing Moira in pain, it made him sick."

Sam had witnessed a birth, had coached another woman through those hours of pain. Another woman... This was why she couldn't be with him, why she couldn't spend any more time with him. Everything he said hurt too much.

"Tell me about Mariah," she said now, needing to get him back to the only thing that could matter.

Her life's work involved helping emotionally devastated people. And she hadn't been able to get that little girl out of her mind. Couldn't bear to have the child living so close, to run the risk of running into her over and over, without finding out if there was something she could do to help.

She wasn't interested for Sam's sake. Never for Sam. But because this was what Cassie did. What made her feel good about herself. What gave her a reason to get up in the morning.

Sam sat forward, his hands hanging helplessly. "Only she could tell us what's on her mind at this point. There were reports of the things that happened during the twelve hours the plane was held captive, but they varied depending on who was talking, where they were sitting. Every report was clouded by the witness's own terror. Not a lot of people noticed the mother and little girl sitting in the back of the plane—"

He paused, then continued. "Brian was beaten up pretty badly—we do know that. Used as an example, the reports said. We're guessing because he was an American. And because he tried to protect his family."

"And Mariah saw that? Saw him…hurt?"

"Who knows?" His eyes met hers, his agony evident. "I'm assuming she probably did. The plane wasn't that big."

"And Moira?"

"They slit her throat."

"Oh, God."

Feeling sick to her stomach, Cassie leaned forward, her elbows on her knees. "In front of the child?"

"We think so. Apparently, Mariah kept crying for a Band-Aid. No one else knew that Moira had been hurt at that point."

"And you said you've had Mariah in counseling."

"Of course. And we've been referred to someone in Phoenix who comes very highly recommended, but at this point, the doctors say that what she needs most is time. And to be surrounded by safety and love."

"She'll get plenty of that in Shelter Valley."

"That's why we're here."

Not for Sam, but for Mariah. He hadn't come back for his own reasons. For his parents or his town—or Cassie.

"I sure could use your help, Cass."

She'd already anticipated his request. "We'll start with Zack's dog, Sammie," she said, her mind hard at work. "But I think it'll probably be best to get her a puppy of her own, one who can be with her permanently. And I'd like to call Phyllis Langford in to help, too. She's a new psychology professor at the U. She's incredibly gifted when it comes to working with damaged emotions—"

Sam stood, grabbed Cassie's hand, pulled her up. "I meant, I could use a friend."

"No." Snatching her hand away, Cassie slipped behind the chair, her hands clutching the back of it.

"I'm not asking for anything else, Cass. Just a friend, someone to talk to."

"We are not, nor can we ever be, friends."

Nodding, Sam headed for the front door.

"Sam?"

"Yeah?" He turned, waiting.

"I'd like to try to help Mariah. Pet therapy might work."

"You don't have to do this for me. Like I said, the woman in Phoenix comes very highly recommended."

"It's not for you, Sam. It's for her." And it was. Almost completely. "We've seen some amazing results in cases like this, where people have been traumatized by other people. Rape victims. Severe spousal abuse. Instances where trust has been irrevocably broken. In such cases, counseling alone doesn't often help, since it's impossible for the patient to trust anyone, including the therapist. But we've found that sometimes these patients can trust an animal, and once trust is reborn, they slowly learn to have faith in people again, too." She paused. "Some people, anyway."

Rubbing his chin, Sam said, "I've never heard of a vet doing counseling before. I'm impressed."

"My undergraduate degree was in counseling," Cassie told him. "I'm fully certified. And I work very closely with a team of psychiatrists from around the country."

"I'm more than impressed." He was proud of her. She could see it in his eyes. Cassie looked away.

"Pet therapy might help Mariah," she said. "What could it hurt to try?"

"Nothing," he answered, his hand on the doorknob. "I'm willing to try anything if it could bring that little girl back to me."

"And back to herself," she whispered.

She saw the agony on his face, and her heart ached for him, this man who'd once been so honorable. Who was now just lonely. And alone.

"I'll talk to Zack and Phyllis, and someone will give you a call."

Sam stared at her for longer than she could handle, and when she glanced away, said, "Thanks, Cass, I owe you" very softly. And let himself out.

He was gone.

She'd survived.

Maybe.

CHAPTER FIVE

FOLLOWING HIS PATIENT out of the examination room, a chart in his hand, Zack Foster grinned. He'd just had the pleasure of telling Shelby's owners that their six-year-old German shepherd was going to be a mother again. They'd been trying for a couple of years.

"Just make sure she's not out in the heat too much," he reminded the man and woman who were taking turns petting Shelby and telling her she was a good dog. Zack hoped Shelby was as happy about the upcoming event as her family was.

"We will, Doctor, thanks."

In her own doggy way, Shelby looked happy. In each of her previous two litters, she'd produced seven puppies, several of them now show-ring champions. She'd mothered them possessively and tenderly.

And speaking of mothers...Zack thought of Randi and what a great mother she'd be. They'd talked about having a baby but hadn't decided on timing.

Zack was already in his thirties, and though he'd

been in Shelter Valley for only two years, he'd already fallen into the town's family-oriented outlook—the larger the better, as far as families went.

Maybe he'd bring the idea up with Randi tonight. A romantic evening... He'd buy her a gift—a new pair of white tennis shoes to go with the twenty other pairs she'd lined up on her half of the closet floor. Maybe a sweatband or two, soften her up a bit. He grinned as he planned his seductive persuasion. Dinner in Phoenix and then—

"Zack?" Cassie called out to him from her office. She wasn't due in until this afternoon. She was supposed to be home catching up on her sleep. Taking care of herself.

His grin vanished. Clutching the chart with both hands, he stopped in her doorway. "You're here ahead of schedule, huh?"

With her crisp white blouse and navy slacks, she was impeccably put together, as always, but she didn't seem at all rested or relaxed. She was pale, and her eyes were hollow and bruised-looking, as if she'd had no sleep.

"Sam came over last night."

Zack's heart dropped. He'd never actually met Sam Montford, but he sure hated the guy. Zack had been the one who'd helped Cassie pick up the broken pieces of the life Sam had left her with.

"If he's giving you a hard time..."

She held up her hand. "Not really. He just wants to be friends."

Zack sank into a chair. "Where was he ten years ago when you needed a friend?"

"In the Peace Corps."

That surprised him. He'd expected to hear that the guy had been partying on a beach in Jamaica. "For ten years?"

Cassie shook her head, focusing on the top of her desk. "For the past couple of years he's been restoring old homes in New Jersey."

"You always said he was brilliant. Had a career in law and politics ahead of him."

"He *is* brilliant. He was attending Montford University on full academic scholarship, and he never really even tried. But apparently he'd rather waste his mind than use it."

"I'm more inclined to believe the man's an idiot," Zack said, not bothering to hide his derision. Years ago, when he and a much younger, more fragile Cassie had spent a lot of time together studying and talking, he'd experienced firsthand the damage the man had done. Montford had taken the life from a lovable, bright young woman and left her little more than an empty body. Back in those days, Zack had fantasized regularly about meeting up with Sam Montford in a dark alley someday.

He was still fantasizing about it.

Sam Montford had a lot to answer for.

Cassie had recovered very slowly, healing physically and emotionally while she found the inner strength to pursue a career. Though she'd very thoroughly and permanently closed herself off from any future romantic relationships, she'd managed to create a successful, contented, *useful* life.

Zack was not going to sit idly by and watch her lose it again.

"His little girl needs help, Zack."

Zack frowned, dropping Shelby's chart on the edge of Cassie's desk.

A couple of nights ago, Ben Sanders, Montford's cousin and Zack's good friend, had told him about Montford's adopted daughter. The details were harrowing, and Zack wasn't sure how much Cassie knew, but ever since he'd heard them, he'd been half afraid she'd want to get involved.

Ben hadn't met Sam and Mariah yet, but Carol Montford had been keeping Ben apprised of family events. Ben had an adopted daughter who was just about Mariah's age and was still recovering from the beatings inflicted by her natural father several months ago. Carol was hoping the little girls would be able to help each other heal.

"She's got a great therapist in Phoenix," Zack said now, having grilled Ben for everything his cousin knew about the situation.

Cassie leaned forward. "She's been in therapy

for almost six months," she said earnestly. "And she's made virtually no progress."

Pushing back from the chair, Zack shoved his hands into the pockets of his jeans. He paced slowly in front of Cassie's crammed bookshelves. Perusing the titles. Retaining none of them.

The situation was delicate, but the answer clear.

"From what I understand, the child was severely traumatized," Zack said. "She might be beyond any sort of help until some of those memories fade."

"But we might be able to reach her." Her voice was full of compassion. And something more. It was the "something more" that made him nervous.

He turned toward her. "You might not make any difference at all," he reminded her gently.

"As long as there's a chance that we can reach her, I have to try. And I want to use Sammie, at least to start with."

Cassie's gaze was strong, steady, unrelenting. Zack knew he'd lost before he'd even begun to fight.

"At what cost to you?" His words were softly delivered; the look he gave her was not. They'd been through too much together, too many dark days fighting demons. He couldn't just calmly let her risk her hard-won hold on happiness on such an unsubstantial possibility.

"How can I measure my own well-being against that of a child?"

Hands on her desk, Zack leaned over until his face was only inches from hers, staring her straight in the eye. "You can't save everyone in the world," he told her.

"This isn't the *world*, Zack. It's my hometown. The town that nurtured me as a child, that has loved me every day of my life. The town that helped me gain back my self-esteem when I thought I had no reason to go on."

Zack held his position. "She's not from this town."

"She's a Montford now."

"And are you sure that that isn't why you're doing this? Because she's Sam's daughter?"

Cassie shook her head. The movement conveniently broke eye contact with Zack. "I've helped people all over this country, Zack, and you know it. I certainly have to do everything I can for someone right here at home."

"For Sam..."

"For *anyone* right here at home. I'd feel the need to make this offer even if she was a total stranger. You know that."

He did. Damn it. Cassie was world-renowned for her innovative approach to emotional therapy—using animals to achieve remarkable results with emotionally traumatized people who'd lost their ability to trust.

"Maybe this one's a little too close to home."

"There's no maybe about that."

He pushed away from her desk with so much force, it moved. Why should Cassie have to risk more grief? Hadn't she already suffered enough at the hands of Sam Montford? Could she survive another assault on her emotions?

"Let me do it," he said, knowing the words were asinine even before they left his mouth. He had no training in Cassie's area of expertise. He was good at lessening the loneliness of old people, at helping a newly blind man find the courage to shower again with a dog by his side, or encouraging a quadriplegic to try to retrain his muscles. He knew next to nothing about emotional disorders.

Cassie smiled, but didn't even bother with a response. Her glorious long red hair was clipped up into some sort of twist, making her look, at that moment, like his fourth-grade teacher.

Arms folded across his chest, he stared at her. "Can you assure me that you won't get hurt?"

"Does life ever offer that assurance?"

Zack stood there for several more minutes before settling back into the chair. "How are you going to do this, Cass?" he finally asked softly. "Seriously, how can you possibly involve yourself with Sam again? In any capacity?"

Her shrug did very little to reassure him. "I just know I have to try."

The sound of suppressed tears filled him with dread.

She was hurting already.

She'd said she was okay, but he knew better. He knew better, dammit, and there wasn't a thing he could do about it.

Except be there to hold the pieces if she fell apart.

SAM, FEELING DISJOINTED, drove his truck slowly into town. He reached for Mariah's hand, the tiny fingers lost in his big, work-roughened palm. "Are you excited to meet your new cousin, honey?" he asked, infusing his voice with a cheer he couldn't really feel. "She's seven, just like you."

Glancing sideways, he smiled at Mariah, willing her to care. If his determination could make something happen, Mariah was going to get well. Sam was sending her every bit of energy, of strength, that he possessed.

How many times in the past seven years had he been discouraged, overwhelmed with the self-hatred that was always there, and found solace in the love of this little girl? Without ever knowing, or trying, Mariah had brought a joy to his life he'd never thought he'd find again.

He'd been there for her conception—or practically, passed out in the very next room. He'd been there for her birth. For every birthday and Christmas. The first day of school. And days in between.

And how many times had he sat with her, wondering if he and Cassie would have made a child as special as Mariah?

Brian and Moira were Mariah's parents, and they'd had the privilege of listening to her childish pronouncements every day. Of being there for her first step. Of chasing her through the house in her pajamas. Of listening to her earnest prayers every night, then tucking her into bed. Drying her tears.

For him, the pleasure of Mariah's company had been, of necessity, occasional. He'd seen the Glory family as often as possible, but sometimes they were away for weeks or months at a time. Mariah always accompanied them, as Moira had accompanied her own parents on the same kinds of trips.

If he'd stayed around long enough for him and Cassie to have the family they'd always planned, he'd have known the same satisfaction as Moira and Brian. If, ten years ago, he'd known the immeasurable completeness a child brought to life, the incredible store of love and excitement, he'd never have left home.

Or would he?

Pulling onto Main Street for the first time since he'd been back, Sam wondered about that. He'd been so unsure of himself in those days, so unsure

of who he was. How could he possibly have experienced—or even understood—the kind of joy
Mariah now brought him?

How could he possibly have been a father, responsible for another life, when he was barely responsible for his own?

"Before we meet your new cousin and her
daddy, we're going to see a statue of my great-
great-grandfather," he told Mariah, slowing the
truck. "Which means he's your great-great-great
grandfather." He lifted their clasped hands, tickling
her neck. Though she flinched, the movement was
almost imperceptible. She certainly didn't smile as
he'd half hoped she might. She didn't even blink.

"I haven't seen it yet, so you and I can see it
together for the very first time, okay?" he asked,
squeezing her hand.

She continued to watch him.

Sam pulled into one of the angled parking slots
along Main Street's curb, got out and helped Mariah climb down. They'd be meeting his cousin,
Ben, and Ben's daughter Alex, in this park a few
minutes from now. And though he didn't really understand why, Sam had very mixed emotions about
the meeting.

Somehow Ben's existence threatened him.

The statue was easily visible from the road, but
until Sam got close to it, it was just a statue that
his mom and dad had told him about. Which was

probably why he was so unprepared for the tremor
that shot through him as he got close enough to read
the inscription, to see the face.

The resemblance was immediately recognizable.
And startling.

The man was a legend. Sam was not. At least,
not in this town.

"Hey, Mariah, do you think he looks like me?"
He lifted her up for a better view.

The child stared at him; she ignored the statue.
She had one hand around his neck, and with the
other, she was clutching the collar of his shirt.

"His name is Sam Montford, too. And since your
name is Montford now, he's related to you, just like
he is to me," he told her, constantly trying to re-
inforce the fact that she wasn't alone in the world.
That she had an entire family surrounding her, loving her, whether or not she let them.

"He's the man who started this whole town," he
explained. Maybe a sense of history would help her.
A story that was enough like one of the books
Moira used to read to the child, to mean something
to her now. To provide a sense of connection. "He
moved out to Arizona from back East; just like
you," he rattled on, repeating some of what he'd
known growing up as the only Montford heir. But
he'd learned much more of his ancestor's history in
the five days he'd been home. The previous year,
Becca Parsons, the wife of Montford University's

president, had spearheaded a project to honor the original Sam Montford, which included a biography, a play and the commissioning of this sculpture. She'd apparently tried to find Sam, to bring him home for the unveiling of the statue, but Sam hadn't left a forwarding address. His phone number had been unlisted.

The only people who'd ever known where to find him were Brian, Moira and the disaster relief organization for which he'd been volunteering the past eight years.

"When your great-great-great grandfather came out to Arizona, he lived with Indians for a while." He gave Mariah the condensed version. The first Montford had been on the run when he'd settled in Arizona. On the run from a stratified society that had killed his dark-skinned wife and biracial son in cold blood.

Mariah didn't need to know about that.

"He met a very pretty woman who was visiting the Indians with her dad, who was a missionary," he went on. "And she was your great-great-great-grandmother."

Looking at Mariah's earnest little face, Sam had no idea if he was getting through to her. Her blue eyes, once so alight with mischief and precocious pursuits, were blank.

"They had several children," Sam said, speaking his thoughts aloud. He looked back toward the likeness of his ancestor, and found himself experiencing a strange sense of pride—of belonging, almost. A *willingness* to belong.

Had that feeling always been there, waiting for him? Or had it been necessary for him to forge his own way, to witness life's extreme sorrows—in the midst of war, famine, earthquake and storm—to appreciate what he'd taken for granted all his life, growing up in Shelter Valley?

Would he ever have found the real Sam Montford if he'd stayed in this town?

"One of their children was my great-great-grandfather. And another one was your uncle Ben's great-great-grandmother."

Sam still couldn't grasp the idea that he wasn't the only Montford heir. He'd been "the only" his entire life. Carol and James's only son. Cassie's only boyfriend. Her only lover. The only Shelter Valley High graduate to score off the charts on the SAT exams. Shelter Valley's only hope for leadership...

"Let's go, hon." Putting Mariah down, he took one last glance at the statue of his namesake and headed farther into the park, holding her hand tightly. "Alex is waiting to meet you."

He spotted Ben and Alex almost instantly, across the park. It seemed fitting that they'd arrived at opposite ends.

"Your uncle Ben's little girl is adopted, too," he

told her. He pondered his next remark, bit it back, then said it anyway. "She was hurt kind of bad, too," he confided, hoping that if Mariah knew she wasn't the only child to suffer, the knowledge might somehow bring her comfort. Hoping that she didn't start to think all children lived happily until the age of seven, when suddenly life turned into hell on earth and you had to wonder why you lived at all. "Alex's mom was married to Ben when Alex was born. She told Ben that he was Alex's daddy, but she wasn't always a very nice lady."

As he repeated the story his mother had related the other night, Sam felt a stirring of compassion for the man he could see across the park, throwing a Frisbee to the laughing little girl who was tripping over her feet as she tried to catch it. "But then later," he continued, walking slowly toward the pair, who hadn't seen them yet, "the man who was really Alex's dad came back from prison—he wasn't a very good person, either—and they made Ben go away and took Alex to a new place. But the new man got mad and hit Alex," he said, praying he wasn't making the biggest mistake of his life.

Sweating suddenly, he had a horrible feeling that he should have spoken to Mariah's counselor before telling her this particular truth. Yet instinct was telling him it *had* to help her to know she wasn't alone.

"Alex called Ben secretly on the phone, and he came and rescued her, and now she's his forever

and ever,'' he said quickly, getting to the good part.
''Just like you and me.''

Ben abruptly stopped his game. He'd obviously
noticed Sam and Mariah approaching. Holding the
Frisbee in his hand, he drew Alex close to him.
Sam's jaw tensed.

''Ready, honey?'' he asked softly, crouching
down beside his daughter.

Mariah buried her face against Sam's neck.

THAT SATURDAY MORNING Carol Montford paced
from her living room across the foyer to the formal
library on the other side and back again, peering
out the huge windows in both rooms toward the
curving drive beyond. Waiting.

She told herself to stop. Went out to the family
room to see if her husband needed help with the
crossword puzzle he was working on. He didn't.
Nor did he want anything to drink—and would she
please just relax and knit or something?

She might have tried to follow his advice. Except
that she didn't knit.

And before she knew it, she'd resumed her path
along the living room windows and through the library.

She so desperately wanted Sam to feel a part of
things again, to know in his heart that Shelter
Valley was his home. To stay.

She was afraid that Ben's being here now would just give Sam another excuse to leave.

She wanted the two boys, the cousins, to find something in each other.

"You have to trust that everything will work out for the best," James said suddenly, coming up behind her at the living-room window, his hands on her shoulders.

Carol slowly covered his hands with her own. Even after all these years, all the heartaches, she still felt a thrill at the simple touch of her husband's hand.

That was all she'd ever wanted for her only offspring. The comfort of loving someone that deeply. That completely. That forever.

"We just got him home again," she whispered, trusting James with her fear.

"But we can't make him stay, my love," he returned softly, unusually solemn. "He has to *want* to do that."

"If he thought we needed him—"

"Oh, no, my dear," James said. She could feel him shaking his head behind her. "You don't want him here out of guilt. Or duty. He wouldn't be happy."

"But what about that precious little girl, James? She needs us!"

"Yes, I believe she does. And I also believe Sam knows that. Your son is an intelligent man."

Carol turned, kissing James on the side of the mouth. "He gets that from his father," she said, tears brimming in her eyes as she worked up the courage to ask the one question no one had yet dared to raise.

"Do you think he and Cassie could ever—"

With one finger on her lips, James silenced her. "Don't, Carol," he admonished. "You'll only torture yourself."

She didn't speak, but after almost forty years of marriage, she didn't need words to communicate with her husband. Her eyes pleaded with him to give her a little hope.

"The boy didn't leave himself any room for reparation," he said quietly. "The damage he did to Cassie was too great to be anything but permanent. There's nothing left for them to go back to."

Carol would still have hoped for a miracle, were it not for the truth she recognized in James's words. Cassie was not the woman she'd once been.

And her Sam was at fault for that.

Because of him, Cassie had been denied any second chances. She would never have a baby, never be pregnant again—because of what he'd done, and what he'd caused to happen, Sam didn't deserve a second chance, either.

AN HOUR LATER, just before lunch, they were back. "How'd it go?" Carol Montford asked, before Sam and Mariah were even fully inside the house.

"Fine."

Sam wanted lunch. And some time with his drawing pad and pencil. Things were changing in Borough Bantam, confusing him. He needed a chance to think it all through, to work out these changes in a way that was beneficial to the village. And to the newcomer, as well.

He needed to find out the newcomer's purpose. His place in the Borough. His long-term intentions.

"How did the girls do?"

"Fine," Sam said again, wanting Mariah to know that she hadn't disappointed him. She'd refused to look at either Ben or Alex the entire awkward time he and his cousin had stood in the park and tried to talk without ever really saying anything. He couldn't let Mariah believe that there was anything wrong with her response. He had to assume it was the only response she was capable of right now.

"Isn't Alex a cutie?" Carol asked, trying valiantly to keep the concern from showing on her aged and still-lovely face.

"That she is."

"And you and Ben, you liked each other?"

"We just met, Mom. I hardly know him," Sam said, wishing he could reassure her. About so many things. The trouble was, he couldn't even reassure himself. He had no idea what the future held.

"But he's—"

"He seemed like a decent man," he allowed, when it became evident that she was going to push until she got some kind of commitment from him.

Carol ran gentle fingers down Mariah's back. "How'd our little one do?' she asked.

"I don't know," Sam said, releasing Mariah's hand and turning her to face her grandmother. "Did you have a good time, Mariah?"

The child stared at him blankly.

"Let me get her some chocolate milk," Carol said, moving away before the little girl saw the hint of tears in her eyes. "She likes chocolate milk."

She *drinks* chocolate milk, Sam amended silently. That doesn't mean she *likes* it.

There's no way of knowing what she likes and what she doesn't.

But for now, the fact that she would drink a glass of chocolate milk was enough.

CHAPTER SIX

ARMED WITH THE ADVICE of psychology professor Dr. Phyllis Langford, and with the instincts that had been serving her well, Cassie let Sammie off her leash in the park Monday morning.

"Okay, girl," she said, squatting down, rubbing the sheltie's ears, "you're on."

There were no rules here, no right ways, no answers. There were only bits and pieces of advice from psychology professionals—not all of it consistent—suppositions and a very few precedents to guide her. And there was her absolute certainty that pet therapy could help where nothing else would. They were breaking new ground. So far, with great success.

Because this was a Monday morning, a school day, the park was deserted. Except for the man walking toward them with his daughter clinging to his hand and staring up at him. Mariah's long black hair was in a French braid. She looked adorable— and fragile—in her yellow jumper and sandals.

"Go say hello, Sammie," Cassie said, her tone of voice changing as she gave the command.

Sammie's ears perked up, she barked once, and off she went, bounding across the park to the two figures drawing closer.

Concentrate on the job, Cassie told herself. *Don't watch the man.* Don't recognize that confident stride. Those long legs that had always looked sinfully good in denim. *Don't even look.*

He was an illusion. No matter how attractive he was, how kind he could be, how gentle and warm. Inside him lurked a man who could be carelessly cruel. A man who made promises he didn't keep.

He stopped in the shade of a palo verde tree—the only tree in this Arizona park—still holding Mariah's hand.

Sammie had reached them, and Cassie's full attention was riveted on the child. Though the sheltie was sniffing her hand, Mariah didn't seem to notice. She didn't look at the dog. Didn't look anywhere but at Sam. Cassie wondered if she was even aware of her surroundings.

The psychological reports had all agreed that Mariah was ''in there'' someplace. That the child's brain was fully functioning. Sam was certain of it, and Cassie was working under that assumption.

Mariah didn't seem to trust people at all. Apparently not even Sam—which was why she didn't dare take her eyes off him. So maybe she'd trust another creature, one who made no demands and required no explanations; maybe she'd trust Sam-

mie. But not unless they could get her focus away
from Sam.

Standing there in her forest-green dress slacks
and white short-sleeved cotton shirt, Cassie continued to watch, waiting for Sam to do as she'd in-
structed him, when she'd called earlier that morning. He'd balked, arguing that they'd been
operating on the premise that only by making Mariah feel totally secure were they ever going to
bring her back. Mariah's counselors thought that
maintaining her attachment to Sam was so important, they weren't even trying to send her to school
yet; they felt she wasn't ready to be away from him.
Cassie knew that. Knew, too, that although Sam left
the child occasionally, Mariah would always sit
completely frozen, in the position he'd left her, until
he returned. And she wouldn't eat for hours afterward. Cassie had spoken about these things with
Mariah's counselor in Phoenix. And at length with
Phyllis.

Cassie's conversation with Sam had been all
business. If he wanted her help, he was going to
have to trust her. And to do what she told him.

He'd eventually said he would.

A minute passed, and then another. Sammie went
on nudging Mariah's hand, sniffing at Sam's shoes.
She pranced around, waiting for someone to notice
her.

"Come on, Sam," she said softly. "I know it's hard, but you can do this...."

Even standing several yards away, she could feel the effort it cost him to disengage Mariah's fingers from his. Could feel the doubt, the pain, even the fear, as though she were experiencing it all herself.

But then, this was Sam. She'd always...felt him.

Holding her breath, she stood completely still, watching as he slowly left the child standing in the park alone. Tears welled in her eyes, but she ignored them. She was working. This was a job. Nothing more.

Ignoring everything but Sam, Mariah reached out her hand to him.

He hesitated, looked over at Cassie, then shook his head, face tense. "I'm just going to run back to the truck to get the picnic basket I forgot," he told Mariah.

Cassie barely heard the words, but she heard the very real compassion behind them.

"You stay here with Sammie," he said to the child. "Her name's just like mine. So you know you can trust her to keep you safe until I get back. I'll just be gone for a few minutes."

Mariah started toward him.

"No!" The sharpness of Sam's word cut into Cassie's heart. God, life was so hard! "I want you to stay here, Mariah," he said firmly. "I'll be back, okay? And if you need anything, my friend Cassie is over there.''

Sam glanced at her, clenching the muscles in his jaw. Even across the distance of several yards, she could read the fierce look in his eyes. *She'd better be right about this.*

Cassie's tears fell when Sam turned abruptly and walked away from his needy daughter.

He trusted Cassie. Trusted her to help this damaged child.

Overwhelmed with sudden despair, she almost called him back. She couldn't handle this. Couldn't go through with it. Couldn't have Sam placing his trust in her so completely. Not when she didn't trust him. She brushed her tears away.

And focused on the child, who stood like a statue, staring at her father's retreating back.

Part of the idea was for Mariah to see that although Sam left, he always returned.

He wasn't going far. But he was going out of her sight. And he'd stay there until Mariah moved. Until she looked somewhere other than where he'd gone.

It might take all morning and into the afternoon.

But unless they taught Mariah that she wasn't as alone as she thought, the child wasn't going to recover. That was the conclusion Phyllis had drawn. One that the Phoenix counselor had eventually concurred with, though she'd believed they hadn't given Mariah enough time to come out of this on her own. She'd reiterated the list of known traumas Mariah had experienced—thankfully, none of them physical—the length of time it could take to recover from them.

Cassie didn't doubt the validity of the professional opinion. She just knew that sometimes animals could help speed up the process. There was scientific proof behind the theories. Though most psychology professionals only seemed willing to try pet therapy as a last resort, they almost all acknowledged that pets were sometimes responsible for lengthening the lives of their owners, for lowering blood pressure. Cassie believed it was just a matter of time until they universally acknowledged that animals could also be used to reach human beings who'd been so injured, so emotionally impaired that they couldn't be reached through normal person-to-person therapy sessions.

"Come on, Sammie, do your stuff," Cassie said, her stomach growing tenser with every passing minute. The child was one stubborn little cuss. Which would serve her well.

Cassie knew.

It had been her own stubborn refusal to die that had brought her out of her dark pit all those years ago. At first, when her own physical health had been so precarious, she'd had her baby to think about. And then, later, when she'd finally admitted to herself that life did go on, she'd found a well-spring of determination she hadn't known she possessed.

Sammie nudged the little girl, but Mariah still didn't respond. She was staring so intently after Sam that Cassie wasn't sure the child knew the dog was there. Wasn't sure she'd notice if the always-blue Arizona sky suddenly clouded over and broke into thunderstorms. Everyone else in town would probably be running outside to gaze up at the heavens. And Mariah would continue to stand there, oblivious, watching for Sam.

Cassie, slowly approaching the child, got close enough to identify any small change of expression on that fixed little face. Was that a hint of fear in Mariah's startling blue eyes? Or was it just a reflection of the bright sun shining down through the tree?

So intent was she on the child's face, watching for any sign of reaction, Cassie didn't notice at first that Mariah's little brown hand had settled on top of Sammie's head. The fingers were moving back and forth from one of Sammie's ears to the other. It wasn't much. Most people would no doubt consider it unremarkable.

But Cassie knew better. She fell to her knees in the carefully manicured grass, not bothering to brush away the tears that rolled down her face. Mariah was taking comfort from the dog at her side.

Thank God.

IT HAD BEEN a long week. And a long day.

Sitting in a lounge chair so comfortable it could have been in the living room, Sam quietly sipped his bottle of beer, Muffy curled at his feet. He was part of the Saturday-night crowd on the back patio at Montford Mansion. But he was having difficulty concentrating on the conversation at hand, and found his thoughts regularly drifting to the ongoing plot of his comic strip.

Yes, it had been a long week, having that first breakthrough with Mariah on Monday and nothing else since. They'd had another session on Thursday. Sam had left Mariah for a little longer, but there had been no new results.

Harder than he'd ever thought possible was being here in town, close to Cassie and not seeing her. Not talking to her. Not sharing her life.

His mother had insisted on this get-together. A little gathering, she'd called it. But it didn't feel little to Sam. Ben and his wife, Tory, and little Alex. Ben's friend and Cassie's partner, Zack Foster, and his new wife, Randi used-to-be-Parsons, whom Sam and Cassie had gone to school with, grades one through twelve. James and Carol. And Sam and Mariah.

He couldn't remember one single family gathering in his whole life without Cassie. She'd always been there.

They'd just finished dinner—steaks out on the grill. A swim in the Olympic-sized pool—though Sam had spent the entire time with Mariah clutching his neck, so he could hardly call it a swim. He and Ben were supposed to be getting to know each other.

The girls were both asleep now—Mariah in a lounge chair on the other side of the patio, Alex in his mother's special guest room, the one he hoped would someday be Mariah's.

Everyone else was sipping drinks, relaxing, talking.

"We should play some canasta," James suggested.

Carol jumped up. "I'll get the cards." She was so obvious in her eagerness to make this whole thing work that Sam felt sorry for her. His mother had always been such a peaceful woman. Content. Secure.

Not this too-attentive mass of nerves, desperate to know that her world was righting itself.

He was completely aware that he was responsible for this, too.

Muffy followed Carol into the house, no doubt hoping for leftovers in the privacy of the kitchen. Sam hoped his mother wouldn't give in to those pleading eyes.

"So how long are you in town, Sam?" Randi asked, interrupting his thoughts. Although the question *sounded* innocent, Sam had a feeling it hadn't been. He was pretty sure Zack and Randi hated him. Couldn't see him gone fast enough.

He tried not to let that get to him. They weren't just his cousin's closest friends—they were Cassie's friends, too. They had a right to hate him.

"I have no plans to leave again," Sam said. He wasn't sure exactly what his plans were, but he knew that much.

Ben sat forward, hand entwined with his wife's. "That's good to hear, cousin," Ben said. "I've been half afraid you were only here for a visit and that you'd be gone before we had a chance to spend any time together."

"Sure you wouldn't rather have the Montford crown all to yourself?" Sam couldn't help asking, though he kept his tone light. "After all, I was the heir apparent all my life. It's your turn."

Zack and Randi shared a glance. Sam suspected it conveyed nothing positive.

"I don't know about that," Ben answered. "But I've come home and I'm glad to be here. I'm also glad to have as much family in my life as there's family to have."

Carol returned, minus Muffy, bearing a deck of cards, and without a pause in the conversation, everyone, a reluctant Sam included, took seats around the big game table in the middle of the patio. Sam was a bit envious of the dog, who'd been allowed to stay inside.

"Sam seems to think there's some *distinction* attached to the Montford name," James said to Ben, as the cards were shuffled.

"A good distinction, right?" Tory asked. Of all the people visiting that night, Sam liked Tory the best. He knew a little about her story—from Cassie the evening he'd gone there. Tory had secrets, things she wasn't proud of. He could sense them. And yet, there was no mistaking the purity of her love for his cousin or for Alex.

"Not necessarily," Sam answered, before his father shared more of his past grievances than Sam was prepared to answer for. "Being a Montford comes with obvious advantages, but it also has its share of hardships."

"Oh, yeah," Zack said with a laugh. "I can see how it'd be a real hardship growing up in *this* house."

"You were always the prince in our fairy tales, Sam," Randi chimed in. "Your life was charmed."

She was right. But it had been a charm he'd never asked for—and in the end, it had come at a cost.

"It wasn't always that easy," Carol said, surprising Sam.

During the years he'd been fighting against a life

he wasn't happy living, she'd been the last person to understand his discontent. To her, everything had always been so clear-cut and simple.

"People expected a lot of Sam. More than any of the other kids in town. He practically lived his life under a microscope."

"Let's get this game going, shall we?" Sam asked.

He might deserve to be the topic of uncomfortable conversation. Had been anticipating it. Figured everyone in town was entertaining thoughts that mirrored Zack and Randi's. But he could only handle the encounters in doses. And without Zack peering hatred at him from hooded eyes.

Because the teams were uneven, Carol was the self-appointed scorekeeper, and Sam conjured up next week's comic strip episode as he played out a few hands of canasta across from his father. The queen in Borough Bantam knew far more than she was revealing. She was on to the newcomer; he'd be wise to watch her, find out what she knew.

As he laid down a red canasta of kings, Sam's mind's eye saw the idiot magistrate, worming his way around his contained little circle, predictable as always. *I am. I am. I am.* And Sam was strangely comforted.

THE NEXT DAY, Sam was in his room working, his pencil flying across the page as the strip he'd envisioned the night before came to life. Mariah was napping on the bed across the room. His parents were in town having lunch with friends.

The bell rang downstairs.

His parents had a housekeeper during the week, but they were on their own on weekends. Which meant that it was up to him to get the door.

The last person he'd expected to see was Zack Foster.

"Hello, Zack." Politeness required that he step back, let the other man inside.

"I offered to stop by as a favor to Cassie," Zack said. "Your mother called about Muffy's allergies, and Cassie told her she'd bring over some Prednisone. Muffy should have one of these every twelve hours until they run out." Zack handed Sam a plastic bottle of pills.

"Thanks," he said. And then, in spite of the fact that he could have cut his tongue out for asking, he said, "Cassie was too busy to come herself?"

"No."

With no one else present, Zack didn't even pretend to like Sam.

"She just didn't want to see me," Sam said, sparing himself nothing.

"Right."

Sam stared at Zack. Cassie's partner was easily a couple of inches taller than Sam. His large athletic frame and blond, blue-eyed good looks would be a definite plus where women were concerned.

Sam had to wonder if Zack and Cassie had been lovers.

Did Zack know about the patch of freckles sprinkled across Cassie's lower back? Did he know that she squirmed and begged when she was kissed there?

"Have you known Cassie long?"

"Ten years."

That long.

Much longer than Zack had known his own wife. They'd mentioned the night before that they'd just met this year.

"Do you know why she's never married?" Sam asked. He'd been so certain that Cassie would be happily ensconced in a huge family by the time he came home.

He'd been prepared to deal with the pain of seeing her living with another man. Loving another man.

He was totally unprepared for the sick feeling of regret he felt for her aloneness. If he really *was* in any way responsible…

"I know why," Zack said, his voice grim.

"But you aren't going to tell me," Sam guessed.

"I don't see that it's any business of yours."

No one in this town thought Cassie was any of his business. This was Shelter Valley, and they took care of their own. He'd deserted; he no longer qualified. Cassie had spent more time here than he had. They'd protect her—even against him. Especially against him. He'd been in town almost two weeks and knew absolutely nothing about Cassie's private life. Not even his own parents were talking.

He clenched his jaw in an effort to keep his mouth shut. Because Zack was right. Cassie's life, her decisions, were *not* his business.

He just couldn't find a way to convince his heart of that.

"Thanks for bringing the pills," Sam said.

Zack nodded, turned to go, then turned back. "I was actually hoping for this chance to get you alone," he told Sam. His belligerence was gone, but in its place was something that bothered Sam even more.

Sincerity.

"Cassie would kill me if she knew I was doing this, but I'm asking you, one man to another, to stay away from her."

A dozen smart-aleck responses sprang to Sam's lips. He uttered none of them.

"This is a small town," he said instead. "We're bound to run into each other. It might make things easier if we could be friends."

"You and Cassie will never be friends," Zack said with certainty. "If she'd been some other girl, from some other place, raised in some other way, she might have been able to get past your screwing around on her, but she isn't and she wasn't. What you did to her cut Cassie to her very core. You don't get second chances when you hurt someone that way.''

''So, if she can't possibly forgive me, if she's always going to hate me, why are you so afraid for me to be around her?'' Sam asked. ''Surely she's immune.''

''You remind her of things she's worked long and hard to forget,'' Zack said, then strode out the door and shut it quietly behind him.

With the truth of Zack's words heavy on his heart, Sam walked slowly back up the stairs. Every time Cassie saw him, she remembered the bad times. The pain he'd caused her.

It was a pain so deep, so cruel, it wasn't ever going to go away.

He and Mariah had another meeting with Sammie that afternoon. He'd have to wake her up soon.

In the meantime, he had a script to write. A fictional town to save.

And he had to figure out how to live in a real town with his ex-wife. A woman who didn't want to see him. A woman he'd never stopped loving…

CHAPTER SEVEN

"Do you mind if I join you, sweetie?" Cassie asked the little girl standing stiffly under the palo verde tree in Shelter Valley Park. "I'm your dad's friend, Cassie. You met me at my work, remember?"

The child didn't even blink as Cassie sat down on the ground next to Sammie. Mariah's hand rested lightly on the dog's head, but she wasn't petting the animal or in any way acknowledging that she wasn't alone.

But they were making progress. Cassie had watched Mariah place her hand on Sammie's head almost the second Sam had left.

"If I'm bothering you or you don't want me here, just let me know," she continued. Sam had been gone for almost ten minutes, and the child's neck had to be getting sore from holding herself so stiffly, watching the exact spot where Sam had disappeared, waiting intently for his return.

Cassie wore denim shorts, a T-shirt with a roadrunner on it, and tennis shoes with no socks. An outfit far more casual than she was used to, but perhaps one that would make the little girl more comfortable.

"I love your outfit," she said, her stomach knotting as she studied the child. She had an hour today. Longer than before. Long enough to force Mariah to focus on something aside from her missing father? Long enough, maybe, to force her to need someone else. "Those shorts are my favorite shade of green, and I really like how the shirt and socks match. You must have bought them all at the same time."

Keeping her head beneath the child's hand, as though understanding the significance of Mariah's gesture, Sammie looked over at Cassie. Cassie could swear Zack's dog was smiling at her. She'd long been impressed by Sammie's sensitivity to emotional undercurrents. Was certain that the sheltie understood much of what was going on around her.

"I think Sammie likes your outfit, too," Cassie confided. "She's listening to us."

Was that a little twitch of her fingers? Was Mariah responding to the conversation? It was impossible to tell if Mariah even listened when people spoke to her. Physically, she could hear just fine; medical tests had determined that. But no one knew for certain how complete her emotional death had been. How shut away she really was. Her catatonic state was most likely a case of the mind protecting itself from an intolerable reality. But how deep did that go? Would she ever be able to release herself from that protection, that silence?

Cassie, pulling her knees up to her chest, continued to chat softly with the child. Telling her about the park she had yet to look at, the children playing around her. Describing her surroundings for her, since she seemed unable, or unwilling, to look at them herself.

Five minutes later, with still no sign of Sam, Mariah's fingers began, almost indiscernibly, to move across Sammie's head. Cassie's stomach fluttered. Those tiny hands seemed so fragile. So helpless and vulnerable. Mariah was too young to have to deal with what life had already heaped on her. She'd seen things no one, let alone a child, should see.

Cassie desperately wanted more for her. Better. Wanted something to take away the anguish.

"I knew your dad back when I was your age," Cassie said suddenly. She shouldn't do this, shouldn't talk about Sam, shouldn't dredge up the memories. It was too risky.

But the words came, anyway.

"I had really long hair then, just like you do—though, of course, mine is red."

Mariah's fingers continued to move slowly across Sammie's head, stroking from ear to ear. Otherwise, there was no response from the girl.

The dog had been sitting still for more than fifteen minutes and would stay in that position until Cassie gave the command to move—even if it was two hours later.

"The boys at school used to tease me about my hair because no one else in our school had hair as bright as mine. And one day, a couple of them came up and pulled the ribbon off the end of my braid and wouldn't give it back to me."

Funny how clearly Cassie could remember that day. How angry and hurt she'd felt by their merciless teasing. And how helpless. They were boys. They were bigger, and there were more of them. There wasn't a damn thing she could do.

She hated that feeling.

"Sam came up behind them and told them that if they didn't give it back to me and leave me alone from then on, he'd make sure they never got served at the ice cream parlor again."

Wrapping her arms around her knees, Cassie smiled. "Of course, he couldn't possibly prevent them from having ice cream, but he believed he could. And because *he* did, so did they. Sam already knew, even that young, the role his family played in this town. He knew he had influence and how to use it..."

She broke off, thinking. Dwelling on a memory she hadn't visited in years.

"You know what was best about him?" she asked, willing the child to look at her. "Back then, he had an unshakable conviction that he could use his influence to the benefit of others.'' She realized she might be talking over the child's head, but she needed to think this through.

He'd really believed, she mused. So when had he stopped believing? It wasn't as though he hadn't accomplished good things after he'd left, but...

Mariah continued to stare off into the distance, where Sam had disappeared. ''Anyway,'' Cassie said, shaking her head, ''the boys never teased me again, and I thought your dad was the most wonderful boy I'd ever met.''

It had taken almost fourteen years for her to find out differently.

Oh, Sam, why? Where did it all fall apart? And why didn't I know?

The fact that he'd never even given her a chance to make it right before he'd destroyed their whole marriage was something Cassie still struggled with. How could she trust her damaged heart to any other relationship, when she knew going in that it could all fall apart without any warning?

Cassie fell silent, watching the child, remembering. Remembering things she'd promised herself never to think about again. She'd lost so much. And what she'd lost could never be replaced.

So had this little girl, standing courageously in front of her.

''Mariah?'' Cassie asked softly. ''We don't

know each other very well yet, but I just want you to know I loved your dad, Sam, very very much. For a long time. And when he went away from me, I felt just like I imagine you do now. Like I couldn't breathe. I couldn't imagine living without him...."

Maybe this was too complex for the child. Too disturbing. Maybe Mariah wasn't listening. But maybe she was. And maybe she needed to hear more than the simple assurances she'd been given to this point. Sam had told her that Mariah had been a precocious child. Maybe she could understand what Cassie was saying.

"But I did manage, honey. And life went on, and eventually I got happy again. And you know what else?"

The child continued to stare off in the distance, blinking only when absolutely necessary.

"Sam came back after all this time," Cassie said. There was no relief for her in that truth. And yet...there was. It meant no more waiting, no more wondering if she'd ever see him again.

Because now she had. It was done.

"So you see, sometimes people have to leave forever—not because they want to, but because it's their turn to go to God. That's what happened with your parents. And Mariah, they loved you *so much*. They still do. It's why they asked Sam to be your dad." Cassie had to stop for a moment as tears threatened. "Honey," she finally whispered. "Sam *will* come back. I promise."

She was watching the little girl, ready to be patient for a year if that was what it took to help her. Mariah was a real beauty. Her features were fine, her skin dusky, her eyebrows black above electric-blue eyes—that were looking straight at her!

Only for a second. A very brief second. But she had looked. For one heartbeat, the little girl had torn her eyes away from that spot in the distance where Sam would reappear and had looked at Cassie.

Yes!

She'd heard what Cassie had said. And she'd reacted!

Jumping up, Cassie had to wrap her arms around herself to keep from throwing them around Mariah. She couldn't wait to tell Sam. And Zack and Randi. And Phyllis, too. Mariah had *looked* at her. Cassie felt good all the way down to her toes.

Sammie was giving the lost, lonely child at least a small measure of security. Without releasing Sammie from duty, Cassie praised the dog, silently promising her a game of Frisbee later.

Then, somehow, she found the means to sit calmly down again and resume her chatter, keeping up a steady stream of banter until she saw Sam heading toward them.

Mariah's hand stayed on the dog's head until Sam was standing right beside her. Her neck craned upward as her eyes followed him. And her hand stole into his.

His eyes met Cassie's and she couldn't help the great big grin she shared with him as she nodded *yes,* to his unspoken question. She'd have to wait until he called her later to tell him what had happened. But for now, at least he knew it had been something good.

Sam and Mariah waited with her while Sammie, off duty, took a turn around the park, squatting a time or two, barking at a bird, running circles around some kids over by the swings.

As she finally parted from them at the edge of the park, telling Mariah that they'd visit again soon, Cassie was still wearing the glow the afternoon had brought her.

For a moment, it had almost been as though Mariah were *their* child and they her loving parents, sharing the unending worry as well as the brief, transcendent joy.

Almost.

But almost didn't count.

And that was where she pulled herself up short. She could care about Mariah. She could help the child. But that was all. This was a job.

Nothing more.

SHE'D KNOWN Sam would call. Had been waiting for the phone to ring most of the evening and was prepared with a ready speech when he did. She was even braced for the warmth of his tone, the gratitude and relief he expressed when she told him what had happened. What she'd been saying when Mariah had responded to her.

What she hadn't been prepared for was his "wait a minute" when she said goodbye.

"What?" she asked, leery now.

"I think we should talk."

"We just did."

"I mean about us, Cass."

Standing there in her soft cotton pajamas, the television droning familiarly in the corner, Cassie curled her toes into the carpet. "We have nothing to talk about."

"We have plenty to talk about," he said firmly. He'd obviously thought about this a lot. And wasn't going to give up easily. Even after all this time, she recognized the determination in his voice.

"I'm not asking for anything from you, Cassie," he went on. "I understand and respect the fact that you want nothing to do with me. But I still think it would be best for both of us if we could just…clear the air."

"I don't think so."

"How can either of us go on until we do?"

She sank down on the edge of the sofa. "I've been going on for ten years, Sam. You get used to it after a while."

"And you can honestly tell me that seeing each other again hasn't changed that?"

Of course it had. How could it not? She didn't answer him.

"I owe you some explanations, at least," he told her.

She heard the guilt in his voice. "You owe me nothing."

"Can you honestly tell me there aren't some questions you'd like answers to?"

Again, she didn't answer him.

"There are things I need to know, Cassie."

"You don't deserve anything from me."

"I know that, but Shelter Valley's a small place. We're going to run into each other from time to time. And we're going to hear about each other...."

He was giving her a chance to tell him what he was eventually going to learn from other people. He wanted to hear about the past ten years of her life from *her*. But there were some things she just wasn't ready to tell him. Things that—at the rate she was going—she might never be ready to tell him. Things he wouldn't hear from anyone else in Shelter Valley. Nobody ever spoke about that tiny grave. Or the tragedy that nearly took her life.

But there *were* things she could say to him. And he was right; there were things she wanted to know. Like, why he'd blown their lives all to hell without even telling her he was unhappy. Without giving

her a chance to help, to fix whatever was wrong.
Why he'd left town without a word of explanation.

If she had some answers, could she finally put
the past to rest?

"When?" she asked him.

"Mariah's asleep. I can come now."

"No."

It was late. She wasn't dressed. She couldn't
have him in her house.

"You name the time and place."

He was going to let her do this her way. Which
made Cassie feel a little more in control. And able
to acknowledge that she didn't want this hanging
over her head for the rest of her life. Able to admit
she wouldn't be getting any sleep that night, wondering what he had to tell her. Imagining his answers to questions she'd been asking for so many
years.

There were very few occasions when he felt comfortable leaving Mariah. And if they did this at
night, there'd be much less chance of anyone in
town finding out about it—and making more of it
than was warranted.

"Okay, now, but not here," she said. "I'll meet
you at the park."

"I don't like the idea of you going down there
by yourself so late at night."

"This is Shelter Valley, Sam," she reminded
him. "And it's only ten o'clock."

"Will you at least promise you'll stay locked in your car until I get there?"

If it would get him off the phone and on his way to get this over and done with… "Yes."

CASSIE'S BLUE TAURUS was the only car parked along Main Street when Sam got there. He pulled the truck in next to her, and met her at the hood of her car.

"Let's go sit on the bench by the sandbox," she said, leading the way without waiting for his answer. Or allowing conversation, either.

The sandbox was new since Sam had left. It didn't hold any memories. He'd have preferred the bench by the palo verde tree.

They'd sat on that bench often during the years of their courtship. During their brief marriage…

The first time he'd taken her to sit there was after she'd fallen trying to beat him in a bicycle race. She'd gone too fast over the curb at the edge of the park. He'd been scared out of his wits when he'd seen her fly off that bike. And so relieved to find that she'd only skinned her knee that he'd made a total fool of himself. He'd told her then and there, sitting on that bench, that he liked her.

She'd laughed at him. "Of course you do, silly," she'd said. "We're friends."

"No," he'd brazened right on, his young heart

too full to keep still. "I mean as in a boy liking a girl."

Astonished, she'd just sat there, staring at him, not knowing what to say. And because he'd been afraid she'd decide she didn't like him back, he'd leaned forward and kissed her.

Just a peck. They'd only been twelve or thirteen at the time. But there'd never been anyone else of consequence for either one of them after that. Certainly not for him. And, he suspected, not for her.

Cassie sat at one end of the bench. The park light across from them revealed the figure-hugging cotton top she was wearing, putting her breasts in a spotlight. God, he ached to touch them again. He'd once had the right to touch those breasts whenever—

Sam swallowed. He'd been wanting her too many years to allow his thoughts to travel that road. Especially when she'd already made perfectly clear that it would be a cold day in hell before Sam Montford ever had his hands on her again.

He sat on the opposite end of the bench. And wondered how to begin, now that they were both here. He'd had so many conversations with her in his mind, explained things over and over, looking for his own understanding by seeing the past through her eyes. Yet now he didn't know how to begin.

"First, I want you to know I've been paying for

what I did to you, to us, every day of the past ten years," he finally said. "I'm so sorry, Cassie. More sorry than you'll ever know."

She nodded. That was all. No words.

Sam hadn't really expected absolution. His sins were too great for that. But God, he'd hoped for...something from her. Some sign of forgiveness.

"I wouldn't have been any good for you if I'd stayed in this town, Cass," he said next. It was a truth he'd come to realize over the years. "I was dying here, and I didn't even know it."

"Dying?" she repeated, staring straight ahead. He couldn't tell if she was really as numb as she appeared, as unaffected, or if she'd just learned to hide her emotions over the years.

"I'm not a lawyer. I never wanted to be a lawyer. Or the mayor of this town. Or a scholar."

"Then why did you say you did?"

Sam blinked. "I didn't ever say that. My parents did. The town assumed I did. No one ever asked me what I wanted."

"You were valedictorian of our class."

"Not because I tried."

"You have a brilliant mind, Sam. How could you not want to use it?"

The old trapped feeling climbed insidiously up his spine. Until he remembered that although he was back in Shelter Valley, back with Cassie, he wasn't the same man anymore. He knew who he was now. What he was about.

Sam watched her shadowed face, wishing he could see her eyes, her expression. "I do use it," he told her. "Just not in the way that was planned for me."

Cassie shook her head. "I don't understand."

"I know. You never did."

"Oh," she said, a trace of bitterness seeping into her voice. "So now it's all my fault?"

"No." The word was soft, filled with grief. "I know it's all mine. I'm just trying to explain, if I can, how everything went so wrong."

"Explain, if you can, why you screwed that...that bimbo."

The harsh words were so completely discordant with the peace of the quiet evening, with the Cassie he'd known. Sam flinched.

"She didn't mean anything, Cass," he said, sickened even thinking about that night. The things he'd done.

He'd never been so ashamed of anything in his life. And had never recovered, either.

"You're the only woman who's ever meant anything to me. You were then. And you still are."

"Don't give me that, Sam," she said. "It's not necessary now. It doesn't matter."

He'd known she felt that way—and he couldn't blame her. But the words cut him deeply.

"As much as I loved you," he continued, because there was nothing else to do, "I knew things weren't good."

"Why?"

Ah. The first bit of emotion in her voice. So she *did* still feel something. Even if it was hate. She wasn't completely immune.

He was a bastard to take satisfaction from that.

"I was never going to be the man you expected me to be. The man you'd fallen in love with."

"And you couldn't tell me this? You had to go out and screw some other woman, instead?"

The verbal slap hit its mark. "I was only beginning to realize the truth myself," he told her. "It took me years to sort it all out."

"I don't understand," she said again.

"I didn't, either, Cass, not for a long time. All I can tell you is that I was ready to explode and I couldn't understand why. I didn't know how to fix it."

"Maybe if we'd talked about it..."

"Maybe." But he didn't think so. They'd both been so young. So set in the patterns their parents had created for them. He wasn't sure either one of them could have figured anything out at that stage.

"So you didn't want to be married?"

Sighing, Sam leaned forward, his elbows on his knees, his hands clasped in front of him. "I didn't know," he told her honestly. And felt a wave of pain when he heard her hissed-in breath. "I knew I loved you to distraction," he said, turning to look at her. "But I felt so *trapped*...."

"I can't believe you didn't tell me!"

"I didn't know what there was to tell. I didn't understand it myself. How could I love you and want out of our marriage at the same time?"

CHAPTER EIGHT

CASSIE'S SILENCE was revealing. She didn't believe he'd loved her.

And Sam couldn't just leave his question hanging.

"I can honestly tell you now," he said, willing her to look at him, and, when she didn't, continuing anyway. "I know with absolute certainty that it *wasn't* the marriage I wanted out of." He took a breath, then another. "But our being married was...connected to everything else. Back then, I couldn't distinguish one thing from another, so I escaped it all. But my problem wasn't the marriage, Cassie."

"What was it, then?" The question was soft, fragile, almost as though she was afraid to hear the answer.

"Shelter Valley. The Montford legacy. The life that had been planned for me. I'm not a desk man, Cass. I can't stand to be shut in all day. I have to be outside. Working with my hands."

She'd turned to look at him, and by the soft light

from the street lamp he saw the disbelief in her eyes.

"You never did manual labor in your life."

"I picked up the bush trimmings when I was little."

"And that makes you a blue-collar worker?" she said incredulously.

"No, but stupid as it sounds, it's one of my fondest memories of being a little kid." He'd found his answers, and now he needed her to understand them, too. Because without her knowing, the outcome of his struggle didn't seem quite complete.

"I get satisfaction from working up a sweat," he went on. Whatever force had sent him running from this town, from her, ten years ago, pushed him now. "I'm good at making things, fixing things," he said urgently. "I look forward to going to work. In a classroom, all I ever felt was the need to get out."

Was she even listening to him? He couldn't tell.

"At night, sitting at our desk in the apartment working on papers for school, I would think about a lifetime of going to the office, reading investment reports. The most physical thing I'd do all day would be to pick up the telephone. And I wanted to jump out of my skin at the thought."

He thought about Borough Bantam, about telling Cassie what he did when he sat at a desk these days, but decided against it. The comic strip was a by-product of the understanding he'd finally, painfully, arrived at. Understanding of himself, of his life.

This wasn't about work. Or success. It was about spending his days doing something that fulfilled him. Manual labor did that.

Besides, Cassie—and the rest of the town— might take offense at his animal portrayals of them. They might not see the compliment he'd intended....

"So our whole life together was a farce," Cassie was saying, her tone abrupt.

"No, it wasn't," he told her, because he couldn't bear the aching he heard in her voice. But in a sense, she was right.

And they both knew it.

ON SOME LEVEL, Cassie wasn't ready to accept what Sam was telling her. Not because she wanted him to put on a suit tomorrow morning and get a corporate job. But because it changed everything.

Every memory she had—the good ones included—would be transformed by this. Would be made unnatural. Unfamiliar. *Different.*

He had to be wrong. He had to be rationalizing a life gone to waste. He was making the best of things, telling himself that he now had what he wanted out of life. To do otherwise was too painful, and there was no way to recover what he'd lost.

"Why didn't you ever remarry?" he asked, when

the silence began to grow longer than their conversation had been.

Rubbing her hands along her thighs, Cassie braced herself. He wanted the truth. And she needed to give it to him. To be free of it. She'd been keeping things hidden inside for so long.

Measuring each word carefully, searching for total honesty within herself, she told him. "You destroyed my ability to trust, Sam." At that moment, there was no bitterness. Just a feeling of calm. "I can't open myself up to that kind of commitment again."

"I can't accept that."

The bench was hard beneath her, but the cool night air was refreshing against her skin. It was already blisteringly hot during the day, but the nights would be pleasant for a while longer. She wished she felt as numbly exhausted as she knew she must be.

"It's not up to you to accept or reject what I say, Sam," she said matter-of-factly. "This is how I feel. End of story."

"One person's untrustworthy, so you've sworn off all men?"

He still faced straight ahead, wasn't even looking at her, but she sensed the emotions churning inside him.

"It was more than that," she said, remembering, barely able to breathe, as she thought back to those first days and nights of their marriage. "You weren't just one person to me. You were my whole life."

Her voice faltered as she resisted her tears. For the first time, Cassie could really talk about the betrayal; for the first time, she was with the one person who would understand. The rush of pain that freedom brought was overwhelming.

A spouse being unfaithful was cruelty. But it wasn't just the sex that had killed her spirit. "You were the good honorable man, the eternal husband, the ultimate best friend." She had to stop. To take a deep breath. To blink away the tears welling in her eyes. "From the time we met, you were the one thing in life I could count on. And I fully believed, I *felt,* I was that for you as well."

"You were."

"No, I wasn't." The bitterness poured out now. She hated it. And couldn't seem to stem its flow. "If I had been, you'd never have been able to do what you did."

"I was drunk."

Cassie shook her head. She'd been drunk often enough to know that excuse didn't fly. "No matter how drunk you were, if I'd meant to you what you meant to me, you would've thought of our marriage. Of us, of *me.* And that thought would have pulled you back."

"I don't agree."

"I'm not asking you to. We're talking about what I know and what I believe."

"But you might be wrong, Cass—have you ever considered that? I was there. I know what I was feeling. And what I wasn't feeling. I know how much you meant to me. Have meant to me all the years I've been away. I *know*." He banged a fist against his chest. "I'm the one who has to live with the emptiness, the regrets, every day of my life."

Her heart started to pound, her blood racing in a way only Sam had ever made it race.

"I know how I felt coming home to you the next day, driving up our street, seeing the front door of our apartment building, remembering the night I'd taken you there for the first time and known it was our home. I carry with me the complete and utter misery I felt the morning after my...disgrace in Phoenix, when I contemplated walking in that door and telling you what I'd done, what I'd destroyed."

He spoke so vividly, his words brought it all back to her. The look on his face when he'd walked in and found her crying on the couch, disheveled, having stayed up all night worried sick about him. She could still feel the shock, the nausea, the dark despair when she'd found out where he'd been. The possibility of another woman had never once crossed her mind. A car accident, some kind of fall, a car-jacking, robbery—she'd even imagined him being bitten by a scorpion or hit by a bolt of lightning. All kinds of crazy possibilities had tormented her that night. But never another woman.

She'd felt a complete and utter fool. Worthless as a woman. As a *person*. She'd given her very soul to another person, thinking they shared everything, and she'd been the only one doing the sharing.

And that day hadn't been the worst of it.

"You have no idea what you lost," she said now, her stomach knotted with bitterness, with remembered despair.

He hadn't just lost *her* that morning. Ultimately, he'd lost their daughter, too.

Not that Cassie didn't blame herself, as well. Her overwhelming desperation, her resulting depression and inability to look after herself, had contributed to the baby's death.

For a moment she considered telling him, but knew she couldn't. Wasn't ready. Didn't have the emotional wherewithal to relive that part of her life. To deal with the emotional reaction that would trigger, the guilt and agony she'd feel.

"I have an idea of what I lost," Sam said after a lengthy pause.

Oh, no, you don't. She shook her head.

Hands on either side of her, Cassie resettled herself on the bench.

He glanced at her. She didn't look at him. But she could feel him watching her, each of them lost in thought.

"You say you lost the ability to trust, Cass, but did you ever try to trust anyone else?" he asked softly. "Another man? Did you even try to see if you *could,* if you could marry and have the life, the family and kids, you always wanted?"

"What I always wanted was you."

"Me and the predetermined life that came with being the wife of Samuel Montford the fourth."

"No, Sam." She shook her head, adamant. "Sure, I was happy with our plans, but they weren't what brought me real joy. That came from the security of knowing that no matter what the world did to us, no matter what happened, we were in it together. I wasn't *alone,* and neither were you. That's what marriage meant to me."

"I felt that way, too."

"Apparently not." She heard her tone of voice and told herself to calm down. "If you'd really felt that way, you'd have come to me that night instead of having sex with another woman. And you'd have stayed around afterward."

Sam sighed. "It's all so confused, Cass. I needed you desperately, yet I knew that if I stayed, I was going to damage the very heart of who you were. I was too messed up to protect you from myself."

Oh. God. Don't do this to me. Don't make me feel you. Don't make any sort of sense. Not now. I can't bear to walk that road again.

"I know we can't go back, Cass, but I'd like to see if we could find something new."

She stood. "No. And this conversation is over, if that's what it's about. I have absolutely nothing to give you, Sam. Nor do I want anything from you ever again."

The earnest look in his green eyes tore at her, and she tried to steel herself against him. "Have you listened to us tonight, Cass?" he asked before she could take a step. "What we have between us is a once-in-a-lifetime chance very few people get. How can we just walk away from that?"

She turned to leave, and he grabbed her wrist.

"Let go of me," she snapped, staring down at his hand.

His grip softened, his thumb almost caressing the sensitive skin on the underside of her wrist. "You just finished saying that what you always wanted was me. For the first time in my life, I have a *me* to give you, Cass."

"That was then, this is now. And if you don't agree to stop talking about this right now, I'm leaving."

He still didn't release her wrist.

"I mean it, Sam."

Sighing, he dropped his hand. "You win." And then, a silent moment later, he said, "I just can't stand the thought of you living your life all alone. Especially since I seem to be responsible."

Though she wasn't sure why, Cassie sat back down.

"It's who I am now."

He turned, pulling up one knee, resting it on the bench between them. Cassie was a little uncomfortable with the closeness, but decided that learning how to ignore him would be the best course. The healthiest course. The course most likely to prepare her for a future of living in the same small town.

"It doesn't have to be who you are, Cassie," he murmured. "You have so much love inside you, so much to give a relationship. It's criminal to let that all die just because I acted like an idiot."

What he said was logical. Unfortunately, logic didn't help.

He tapped her thigh, once, lightly. "The world is full of good, trustworthy people."

Cassie squirmed. "I know."

Silence hung between them again. She took deep calming breaths, trying to rein in the emotions he was unleashing. She couldn't believe, after all this time, that she was actually sitting here in Shelter Valley with Sam. Couldn't believe that any of this still mattered.

And yet...it did.

"It's kind of ironic, you know?" he said suddenly.

She swung her head around to meet his half-smiling gaze. "What?"

"You want to teach Mariah to trust again, when you don't believe in it yourself."

There is a big difference, dammit!

"Don't you see a pattern here?" he asked. "You've dedicated your life to a new therapy whose entire purpose is to reach damaged people and teach them to do something *you* can't do."

"I work with victims."

"And you weren't one?"

Coming from him, from the man who'd caused her the lifetime of heartache and grief, the statement had a debilitating impact.

She *felt* like a victim.

"It's not other people I'm afraid to trust, Sam," she blurted.

"You said it was."

She shook her head, looked out into the darkness in front of them. "No, I said you destroyed my ability to trust."

"Same thing."

"No. It isn't." She needed air. And the deep breath she took didn't give her nearly enough. "It's myself I don't trust."

The words, spoken aloud, were frightening. She'd never said them before. Never really allowed herself to think them. But she'd known.

"I don't understand."

"I let myself down. I was partly responsible for what happened to me and..." Her words trailed off.

Elbows on his knees again, hands clasped, Sam contemplated her for a moment, then asked, "How? And what's that got to do with trust?"

"Because I chose to love you, to give you every single part of me. I held nothing back, had nothing in reserve to see me through without you. I had nothing left because I'd given it all to you." She exhaled shakily. "That's why I can't trust myself in another relationship. I can't trust my judgment, can't trust myself to see when something isn't right. I can't trust myself not to give away everything I have—again. I just can't risk it. That's what I mean by letting myself down."

Sam straightened immediately, his back rigid. "That's *not* letting yourself down!" His voice was loud. "That's the purest form of love, Cassie, the kind God must have intended for all of us to share. And by offering that, you opened yourself up to the purest form of joy."

"I must've missed that part," she said wryly.

"No." He shook his head. "I missed it. Or rather, I let my own inadequacies get in the way. It's not your fault, Cassie. I blew it."

"Of course you did." She glanced at him, and then away. He was too damn close. "But before then, I blew it, too. I made the choice. I turned myself over to you lock, stock and barrel. I made a bad judgment call.'' She paused, wet her dry lips. ''My instincts told me I could trust you completely, Sam. They were wrong, and it cost me dearly. I can't afford to give them a second chance.''

They sat silently for a while, each looking out into the night. Some detached part of Cassie wondered which of them would get up first. Wondered why she wasn't already home, getting some much-needed rest. She had a long day tomorrow.

Church. Which would be hard with all the tongues wagging due to Sam's return. People were going to be watching her. Wondering. Some good-hearted souls who still believed in happily-ever-after would be looking for signs that she and Sam had found their way back to each other.

Others would be waiting to help if it looked as if she was going to fall apart again.

With her family on their extended trip, she'd been sitting with the Montfords at church. She'd have to sit alone tomorrow.

And then, after church, she'd have a full day at the clinic, still playing catch-up because of her time away. This next week she was supposed to submit an article to a worldwide professional journal, and she couldn't afford to pass up the opportunity. It wasn't a veterinary journal, but a psychology one. She'd been invited to write an analysis of pet therapy as an accepted form of trauma counseling.

Sam broke the silence. ''You know, after I left

Shelter Valley, I wandered around the country for a little while, doing odd jobs.''

She didn't want to know.

"When I first started out, I was determined to make it on my own, not to use one dime of Montford money. But that was too easy. It didn't take me long to figure out that life had to be about more than I'd realized. Somehow, I was missing the big picture, but I had no idea where or how to find it. Soon after that, I signed up for the Peace Corps. And that's where things started to become clear to me.''

In spite of herself, Cassie listened, hearing far more than his words were telling her. She could feel his struggle. Was there, struggling with him.

"Some of the things I saw would make you physically ill.''

"The deprivation, the filth and disease, the atrocities. The children whose bones protruded due to malnutrition. The barbaric medical practices.''

He paused, rubbing his hands together as though washing them.

Washing away disturbing visions?

"Those things taught me very quickly to measure life on a different scale. When you're standing in the middle of a town that's little more than dirt paths and falling-down shacks and you're among people clothed in things we wouldn't consider good enough for rags, and you watch the joy on their

faces as they witness a marriage between two of
their own, you know that all the wealth in the world
can't buy what matters most.''

His voice slid across the cool night air. Touched
her. This was her friend. The man she'd grown up
with, the man she'd once known as well as she
knew herself. She was nineteen again, soaking up
his every word.

Every time Sam had talked to her like this, she'd
felt more complete. Right with her world. She
couldn't let herself feel that now. She just *couldn't*.

''But according to you, we had that kind of
love,'' Cassie said. She had to freeze up inside. It
was either that, or crumple.

She started to cry, and looked away.

''That was only the beginning of my journey,''
he told her slowly. ''I helped rebuild that village
before I left. And although I missed you constantly,
for the first time I went to bed at night feeling *good*
inside. I'd done something worthwhile.''

''You did worthwhile things here.''

He shook his head. ''I ran for student council,
fought for better food in our high-school cafeteria.
I visited a few nursing homes, participated in fund-
raisers like that leukemia foundation thing, and got
good grades. None of that compares to saving lives.
To providing a decent way of life where there is
none—digging proper wells for clean water, build-

ing a school or medical clinic, planting crops. It was *real,* Cassie. Not like what I did at home.''

''You were just a kid here, Sam,'' she said. She had no idea why it was so important to fight him on this. ''Had you lived in Shelter Valley as an adult, you'd have accomplished a lot more than cafeteria food and fund-raising.''

''But I wouldn't have gone to bed at night bone-weary from a day's labor. I never would have experienced the feeling of lying down, knowing I'd done what I was meant to do. Knowing, for that one day, I'd done all I could.''

Threatened but not sure why, Cassie didn't argue with him anymore.

''Anyway,'' he continued after a few minutes, ''when I got back to the States with Moira and Brian, we signed up as volunteers for a national disaster relief organization. Any time of the day or night, any time of the year, we'd get calls, and within hours we'd be on a plane to someplace where a tragedy or disaster had occurred. We'd attempt to fix things. To save people. To clean up. To put lives back together. Years of that teaches you many things, Cass—and one of them is that as long as there's breath, there's hope for a second chance.''

He'd caught her, and she hadn't even seen it coming.

"I'm leaving." Rigid, frightened, crying, she walked quickly away.

But she wasn't quick enough. His "I can't give up on us, Cass" hit her before she made it to the safety of her car.

And stayed with her all the way home.

MARIAH WATCHED Sam as they drove to church on Sunday morning, but she wasn't thinking about breathing right then. Sam had said the church was God's house. She'd never been there before. Sam said he didn't go much, either, but that if they went, it would make Grandma and Grandpa happy.

She didn't know about that. Seemed kind of mean to make them happy because that would make the sadness worse. The way she figured it, if you didn't know happy, you couldn't know sad. Seemed kind of dumb of Sam not to have figured that out yet. But he would. He was a smart man.

As smart as her daddy had been. And her daddy hadn't been able to make the bad men stop. Hadn't been able to keep the sad things from happening. He couldn't tell Mariah to be quiet so they wouldn't hurt him anymore, or hurt her mommy. She hadn't meant to cry out loud like that....

She wasn't too sure about going to this house that belonged to God. Except that the lady Sam called Grandma said it was a place to talk to God, who lived in heaven. Mommy lived in heaven, too,

and she really, really wanted to talk to Mommy
again. To see if she was breathing and…and if her
throat had stopped bleeding. It was okay if Mommy
didn't want to live with Mariah anymore. Heaven
must be very nice, and someone would want to stay
there. Mariah understood about that. She just
wanted to see Mommy breathing.

And Daddy, too.

Everyone kept saying Sam was her daddy now.
Even Sam. And that her name was Montford, not
Glory.

She liked Sam a lot—but he was Sam. And her
daddy wasn't breathing. And she didn't want Sam
to stop breathing, either.

"Why are you frowning, honey?"

Mariah waited. Okay. It was all right. He'd
breathed again. She hated it when Sam talked. She
couldn't see breaths when he talked, and that scared
her. If Sam ever quit breathing, if he went away…

For just a second, she thought about Sammie.
The dog. Could he be at God's house, too?

Sammie was the best dog Mariah had ever
known.

She thought about Sam's friend, Cassie, who had
a nice voice. And told a story about Sam that Mariah was still guessing about.

Maybe Sammie would be at God's house and
would sit next to Mariah. That wouldn't be bad.

Sam was still breathing….

CHAPTER NINE

"HEY, YOU TWO MIND the interruption?" Sam asked his parents Sunday night. They were in bed, reading, as they'd done every Sunday night of his boyhood.

It was reassuring to find them still doing so.

"No, son, come on in." James laid down the book he'd been reading. *Standing For Something.* Sam read the title as he settled on the end of their four-poster bed, pulling his foot underneath him.

"Good book?"

"So far," James said. "I picked it up because the forward's by Mike Wallace from "Sixty Minutes." I figured anything he was endorsing had to be interesting reading."

His mother closed her book of poetry, setting it on the nightstand along with her reading glasses. "What's on your mind, Sam?"

Sam shrugged. He'd rather talk about his father's book another minute or two. "Did you read on Sunday nights all the time you were in Europe, too?"

"You can't have come in here just to ask us that," Carol said. And James followed with, "Of course we did. Anytime we were in for the evening.''

Sam nodded, tracing the quilted pattern on the white bedspread with his index finger. They were both watching him, waiting. Carol was frowning, James withholding obvious concern until he'd heard what Sam had to say.

He looked up at them. ''I've been starting to make some plans and I wanted to keep you apprised.''

Burrowing out from under the covers, Muffy shook her head, tags jangling. Her entire body quivered, and Carol pulled the dog onto her lap.

''So what are they?'' James asked.

It had been so easy when he'd tried out this conversation in the shower that morning. He'd come home ready to be the man he really was. So why did he suddenly feel like a little boy again? A Montford boy, with all the responsibilities and expectations the name entailed.

''I have to be here pretty constantly right now, for Mariah's sake, but I can't just sit around and do nothing all day.''

Tears sprang to Carol's eyes. ''You aren't leaving.''

''No.'' Sam wished he could ease the fears he'd planted so deeply inside her. ''Not unless you're kicking us out,'' he said.

James quietly took his wife's hand. ''The house

may be ours to live in as long as we're alive, but you know darn well it's yours, Sam. Yours and Ben's. We couldn't kick you out if we wanted to.''

''Not that we ever would,'' Carol assured him swiftly, wrapping her fingers around James's.

Envy of their closeness, their intimacy, coursed through Sam. But so did contentment. It felt good to come home from a world gone crazy, to find his parents still very much a team. Very much in love.

''You want to start going down to the office?'' James asked. ''I turned everything over to Lyle Simmons before your mother and I left for Europe, but I'm sure he'd be glad to have you taking an active interest in the business.''

Lyle had been his father's righthand man for most of Sam's growing-up years. He ran Montford, Inc., one of the nation's most prestigious investment firms, and he probably ran it better than Sam could ever have done. That was partly because Lyle loved doing it, and Sam never would.

The old trapped feeling started to emerge, but Sam shoved it away. ''I'm not joining the business and I'm not going back to school, Dad,'' he said firmly. There wouldn't be any discussion about this.

''Okay.'' James nodded. Carol looked from one to the other. With her free hand she was slowly petting Muffy.

''I have no intention of being a lawyer.'' Even though two previous generations of Montfords had gone into the legal profession. Including his father, who hadn't even wanted to practice law. He'd opened Montford, Inc. shortly after passing the bar exam.

"I think, after all that's happened, your mother and I have already figured that out," James said, a hint of a grin on his lips.

Okay, so maybe he was coming on a little strong. Rather like the know-it-all fifteen-year-old he was trying not to be.

"What *do* you want to do?" Carol asked softly, her eyes filled with concern.

He looked closely, but didn't see any disappointment there. Maybe the years had changed them, too. Or shown them alternatives that hadn't been clear all those years ago.

He could tell them about Borough Bantam. Perhaps he should. Only that morning, he'd seen his mother reading the strip in the Sunday edition of the Phoenix paper. But it was too important that they accept the man he'd found himself to be. The man who would rather fix cars in a garage than count money in a bank. The success of Borough Bantam was a fluke. It was great. But he'd been just as happy building roads in Illinois before he'd ever begun to even think about marketing the comic strip.

That, actually, had been Moira's idea.

And once the strip had become successful, she'd

urged him to take advantage of all the attention the press wanted to give its creator. Sam had adamantly refused. He'd carefully avoided any mention of himself at all. His publisher, accepting that he wasn't going to budge, had decided to play on the mystery element, instead. No one knew who S.N.C. was.

"I'd like to open a business renovating homes," he said. "It would have to be on a part-time basis to begin with, until Mariah recovers, but I'd like to start with some of those old homes down by the cactus jelly plant. They've become awfully run-down in the time I've been away."

"People started moving closer to town," James said. "The value of the houses dropped, but that allowed some of the farm workers in the area— cotton-pickers and field laborers—to buy them. Gives these people a solid base from which to raise their kids, send them to school."

"But they can't afford to keep the places up as well as they'd like," Carol said.

"So I'll help them."

"They can't afford to renovate, Sam."

"I'll work cheap," he said. "I wouldn't charge them anything if I thought they'd let me get away with that."

"They've got their pride."

"So let's give them something else to be proud of." Sam was eager to get started. And delighted to see that his parents weren't falling all over themselves to talk him out of his new venture.

Or into a different one.

"I can set them up on payment plans, ten dollars a month if need be. And I'll enlist their help as much as possible—work *with* them, not for them." There would be real satisfaction in that, as there'd been in his Peace Corps assignments and in disaster relief. He didn't need these people's money. What would he do with it, anyway? Except donate it someplace.

His share of the ever-growing Montford fortune aside, he made enough off the now nationally syndicated Borough Bantam to keep them all quite comfortably.

"You know how to do all this?" James asked. "The plumbing, electrical, woodworking, everything?"

His dad sounded impressed. Sam had never even considered that possibility.

"I do." He nodded, almost embarrassed. "I told you about renovating those homes in New Jersey, but I also spent a winter learning the plumbing trade. Another eighteen months with an electrician. Another eighteen months in total doing mechanic's jobs. I've got certification in all of those trades. Oh, and I built roads, too."

Carol still seemed bemused. "Why, Sam?"

He met her gaze. "Because it felt right."

They talked a while longer, his parents asking questions that Sam was happy to answer. He'd liked the renovating work best of all—finding the perfect fixtures to match the time period of whatever house he was working on. Discovering the exact trim for an old wooden farmhouse, or a claw-foot tub to fit a Victorian-era bathroom. It had been like putting together a big puzzle full of history and family memories.

"So you're really home to stay?" Carol asked, when the conversation finally wound down.

"Yes." Sam had never been more sure of anything.

The pattern in the bedspread interested him again. A lot. "I have something else to tell you," he said.

"About Mariah? Or her poor parents?" Carol had already put pictures of Moira and Brian in the Montford family photo album. She'd tried to get Mariah to help her, and when the child had simply sat, staring at Sam, she'd kept up a steady monologue, describing every photo so Mariah could share in the event, anyway. Assuming Mariah was listening….

Sam shook his head. "About Cassie."

"What about her?" Carol's voice was suddenly sharper.

"You haven't done anything to her, have you?" James asked gruffly.

"Hey." Sam held up both hands. "I surrender!"

"We're sorry, Sam," James said, sharing a sideways glance with his wife. "That girl's had some pretty rough times. She doesn't need any more."

Sam's parents felt responsible for what he'd done. He had no idea why that fact hadn't occurred to him before. He'd always known he'd hurt them, disappointed them. He hadn't realized he'd also shamed them.

But he *should* have known. He knew them.

"I have no intention of hurting her," Sam assured them.

Carol leaned forward, touching his face with one gentle hand. "Your presence here has got to hurt her, Sam. But she's a strong woman, and she'll be able to deal with that. All I'm asking is that you be sensitive and stay out of her way as much as you can. Make things easy on her."

Sam felt the muscle in his jaw twitch. "I told her last night that I intend to try to get her back."

Carol gasped.

"No!" James said immediately.

Carol glanced over at him, and though Sam couldn't translate the quick conversation that took place, he had a feeling his mother was begging his father for a chance to hope.

He felt better already, knowing he'd have her on his side.

"Promise me you'll stay away from her, Sam,"

James said. He looked older as he leaned back against the headboard. Old and tired. As though he'd aged in the past five minutes.

Sam swallowed. How did a man forgive himself for all the damage he'd done? The anguish he'd caused to those he loved?

How did he ever make restitution? Was it even possible?

"I can't do that, Dad."

Carol wrapped both arms around Muffy, watching Sam and his father.

"You owe it to her, to all of us—"

"I owe it to her to try to bring back the person I know is still living inside of her," Sam said fiercely. He'd felt their connection last night. Only briefly. But it had been there.

And Cassie had felt it, too.

Carol's eyes were wide. Worried.

Swinging his feet to the floor, James sat on the edge of the bed, a hand on either side of him. He was staring at the wall. "There are things you don't know, Sam. Things that make it impossible for you and Cassie to ever go back."

"I know she's sworn off relationships," Sam told him. "We had a long talk last night, and she told me about her inability to trust. I believe trust is something we can reestablish."

"Sam..." Carol began.

"It's okay, Mom," he said, standing, one hand

on the cherry-wood post at the end of their bed. "I know I have my work cut out for me, but who better than the person who betrayed her trust, to give it back?"

"There are some things you can't give back, Sam. Some things that can't be fixed." James stood, too.

"Maybe, but this isn't one of them."

"You don't know everything."

"I know what I have to know."

"Did she tell you anything else, Sam?" Carol asked softly, both hands buried in Muffy's fur. "Anything about that time after you left?"

"I know it was really hard for a while."

"Specifically," Carol said. "Did she say anything specific?"

Sam thought back to the night before, trying to remember exactly what Cassie had said. And realized that it had been relatively little.

It was what she *hadn't* said that had spoken to him the most. He'd sensed that the only way she'd ever be healed was to find what she'd lost. And he was the only one who could help her do that.

No matter where life took them, no matter what they suffered, they needed each other. They always had.

"I guess not," he finally admitted. "Nothing specific."

"Well, there are things you don't know," James said again. His eyes were sad, almost...pitying.

Sam's heart beat faster. "What things?"

James shook his head. "They aren't for us to tell you, Sam. If and when she wants you to know, she'll tell you herself."

His head swung toward his mother. He couldn't accept that. She had to tell him.

"I'm sorry, Sam." Carol shook her head, too. "It has to come from Cassie."

"Is she ill?" he asked, his voice tense. "Has she got some kind of disease?" She couldn't have. She looked healthy and fit. But tired. Alarm shot through him. Was there a reason for that fatigue other than overwork?

"No disease," James said, dispelling that particular fear. "And we're not saying anything more. Just forget about the two of you ever getting back together. It's no longer possible."

His father's warning came too late. Sam had already made up his mind.

CASSIE AND SAMMIE saw Mariah in the park twice more that next week. Although there was no new progress—and that in itself was a step backward—Cassie still believed they were on the right track. That they had a chance of reaching the child. Mariah always stood beneath the palo verde tree and

stared after Sam. She didn't speak or show any sign
that she was listening to Cassie.

But Cassie couldn't give up hope. She continued
to talk to the child. Telling her about Sam when he
was a boy. About some of the escapades the two
of them had gotten into. Like the time they'd
ditched school to dig for gold, and she'd fallen in
the stream and caught a cold, which turned into
pneumonia. They'd only been about ten. Sam had
gotten his hide tanned.

She probably would have, too, if she hadn't been
so sick. Instead, she got spoiled.

Each day with Mariah, she ended her monologue
with the statement that there were some things in
life you could count on. Like Shelter Valley. It was
always there. For more than a hundred years, Shelter Valley had survived one crisis after another.
Lack of water. Too much rain. Mountain lions. Ma-
rauding javelinas. A tornado. And always her people were steadfast. Helping each other in whatever
way was needed.

As long as Mariah was in Shelter Valley, Cassie
told her, she'd have friends.

Mariah's position, facing the direction Sam had
left, never changed. Cassie wondered how the child
had the self-control to be so still; most seven-year-
olds couldn't sit still for two minutes.

Mariah's lack of response didn't change, either.
No matter how much Cassie spoke to her, how

many times she tried to get the child to look at Sammie—or a bird or other children or a tree—it was as though Mariah didn't hear her.

But what did change, finally, was Mariah's body language. The child wasn't so rigid the following Thursday afternoon. Her spine was more relaxed, her shoulders not quite so stiff. And the fingers tangled in Sammie's fur were moving constantly.

There was nothing tentative or noncommittal about the child's communication with the dog. Mariah didn't look at the dog, but caressed her from ear to ear, back and forth, burying her fingers in Sammie's fur. She was using her sense of touch to connect with the world.

Sammie sat grinning, her tongue hanging out of her mouth, basking in the attention.

Cassie wanted so badly to hug the child, she crammed her hands into the pockets of her navy slacks, her elbows pushed against her sides.

Sam noticed right away that there was a change, when he came to collect Mariah. Even before he got close enough to take the child's hand, Cassie saw him watching Mariah's fingers. Then he looked at Cassie, brows raised, mouth stretched wide in a smile.

"I'm making the old apartment over the garage into an office," he told Cassie as he followed her to her car that afternoon. He'd told her on Tuesday afternoon about his venture in the house-renovating business.

Cassie tried to busy herself with Sammie, getting the dog to the car and then inside. But Sammie was too damn good to need any prompting. The dog would probably find a way to open the car door herself if Cassie forgot to do it.

"I've already got a couple of suppliers lined up, referrals from some of the folks I worked with back east. I figure it'll only be a couple of weeks before I'm ready to find my first project."

She didn't want to know this. Confused by him, by herself, she shut the door behind Sammie and walked around to her side of the car. "We can come here again on Saturday?" she asked Sam.

"Of course."

Their eyes met, held, until Cassie looked away. She focused on her charge, on the only thing that mattered. "It was great seeing you, Mariah," she said. "On Saturday, maybe we can get Sammie to play Frisbee with us. She looks really funny running around with that thing in her mouth."

Mariah was staring at Sam's shirt. She didn't blink.

AFTER DROPPING Sammie off, feeling guilty for being glad that Zack and Randi weren't there to ask questions, Cassie drove straight to Phyllis Langford's house. Her new associate—and friend, Cassie thought—had told her to stop by anytime. Cassie was hoping she'd meant it. Hoping the psychology professor was at home.

Phyllis *was* home and seemed glad to see her. Cassie found herself sitting at the kitchen table, a glass of iced tea in front of her, before she had a chance to change her mind about being there.

"I need some advice," she said, as soon as Phyllis, dressed casually in cotton shorts and a knit top that showed off her trim waist, was seated across from her.

"I kind of thought so," Phyllis said, grinning. "Shoot."

Cassie frowned. "I'm that obvious?" She'd taken great comfort in her ability to hide from the world. Hated to think she was really so transparent.

Hell, the whole town would be pitying her if they had any idea how messed up she felt right now.

"Not at all," Phyllis said. "I've just had enough experience to recognize the look. So what's up? Mariah?"

"Partly." Cassie told Phyllis about the five visits they'd had so far. The slow progress. "I didn't want to call her counselor in Phoenix yet," she confided. "She wasn't all that convinced there was any point in doing this, and I don't want her to pull the rug out from under us, especially when I still think we have a chance to make this work."

"There's no reason to call her unless you notice

some worsening in the child's behavior,'' Phyllis assured her. ''Mariah's having her biweekly meetings with the woman, right? If there's a problem, the doctor will catch it.''

Cassie took a sip of tea. ''Am I kidding myself, here?'' she asked Phyllis.

''In what way?''

''I don't know.'' Cassie pushed a strand of hair out of her eyes. Her twist had come loose while she was in the park with Mariah. ''Maybe I'm looking for something that isn't there, taking hope where there really isn't any.'' She gazed across at Phyllis. ''I mean, she's moving her fingers, and that's it.''

''It's a step, and when you're dealing with something like this, every step counts.''

''You don't think I'm getting too personal to be objective?''

Covering Cassie's hand with her own, Phyllis shook her head. ''There's no such thing as 'too personal' with what you're doing, Cassie. Your work with Mariah is all about getting personal.''

Sighing, Cassie looked down. ''You'd think I'd know all of this by now. Anyone might have the impression, that this was the first case I'd ever worked on.''

''I think there's more going on here than a case,'' Phyllis said gently. ''You're not losing your objectivity where Mariah's concerned. What you *are* losing is trust in your own professional judgment.''

Phyllis's words hit her hard. Were the insecurities going to infiltrate her work now, too? It was the one thing she'd always been able to feel completely confident about. She was a pioneer in her field. She knew the value of her skills.

"So, you want to talk about what might be getting in your way?" Phyllis asked gently. She gave a great deal of attention to her glass of tea, stirring methodically, adding sugar, stirring again.

"I'm not certain that full recovery is imminent, but I feel convinced that we're helping Mariah," Cassie said slowly, stirring her own glass of tea. "What I'm not sure about is *my* ability to survive her therapy."

CHAPTER TEN

CASSIE SAT in Phyllis's kitchen, an educated professional, world-renowned in her field, feeling like a kid who needed her mommy.

"I'm losing control," she told Phyllis. "Having Sam around is undoing everything I've done to get myself grounded over the past ten years. So much for being an emotionally stable woman, in charge of my own destiny."

"You *are* stable," Phyllis said firmly, leaning her forearms on the table. "The fact that you're here, talking to me, means you're in charge. You aren't helpless. You haven't buried yourself in the past, or forgotten the lessons you've learned. Yes, you're having a tough time. You're feeling off balance and that's a natural and appropriate response under the circumstances. But instead of giving in to despair or bitterness, you're fighting back."

Cassie shrugged, a bit embarrassed. "You make me sound...impressive."

"If you could step outside yourself, see what I've seen in the short time I've known you, heard what I've heard from people who love you, I think you'd be surprised at what you'd find.'' Phyllis held Cassie's gaze. ''You're helping Sam's daughter in spite of your past history, and that alone says what a remarkable woman you are.''

Looking over at the other woman, a redhead like herself, Cassie smiled tremulously. And tried to let herself believe what Phyllis was saying.

''I've been telling Mariah stories about Sam, incidents from when we were younger, trying to build a sense of continuity for her in Shelter Valley,'' she said after a while.

''And also a bonding tool for the two of you,'' Phyllis added.

It was something Phyllis had suggested to her in the first place. To find such a tool.

''Yeah, well, it may or may not be helping her bond with me, but it's sure making it hard to keep my distance from Sam. I've got him coming at me from one side every time I see Mariah, telling me about his plans, giving me updates on his activities. And I've got the past coming at me from the other side as I relive it all for Mariah.''

''What do you think you should do?''

''Move.'' Cassie attempted a grin.

''It's your turn to run away, huh?'' Phyllis asked.

''Of course not. But I'm human. You've got to admit, from my point of view it's a tempting proposition.''

''I can see that it would be.''

"So what do I do?" Throat dry, she sipped her tea.

"What do you *want* to do?"

It wasn't a question Cassie asked herself very often. "I want to quit hurting," Cassie answered.

"I know," Phyllis replied, her eyes filled with compassion. "Believe me, I know."

Cassie studied the woman, the tremors around her mouth, the pain in her eyes. "It sounds as if you really do."

"My ex-husband was unfaithful to me, too." Phyllis's eyes were shadowed.

"Oh." And then she added, "Did you just want to die?" It had taken Cassie a long time to get over that feeling.

"At first," Phyllis said. "And then I wanted him to."

Running a finger along the rim of her glass, Cassie blinked back tears. "Me, too."

"We'd been married for four years, and we both had successful careers. I thought we were on the right track...."

"What happened?"

Eyes moist, too, Phyllis shrugged apologetically. "He was intimidated by my intelligence. He hated when I analyzed things. And he was threatened by the fact that I understood him so well."

Cassie and Sam hadn't had any of those problems. "He told you all this?"

"No." Phyllis shook her head. "He just salved his ego with a leggy brunette from the PR department. I figured out a lot of it afterward. At the time, I knew something wasn't right, but I assumed it was because of our job demands, that sort of thing. And then, one weekend when he was supposedly out of town on business, I ran into him and his brunette at a restaurant in downtown Boston—which is where we're from."

"What did you do?"

"Gained almost fifty pounds." She smiled sadly. "Not that night, of course, but over the next year."

Cassie leaned over to look up and down Phyllis's trim frame. "What were you before, anorexic?" she asked.

"No." Phyllis laughed. "Since I came to Shelter Valley last summer, I've been working on a weight-loss program with Tory Evans. You know her, I think—she's married to Sam's cousin Ben."

"We've met several times," Cassie said.

"Tory's older sister, Christine, was my best friend. She was killed last year in a car accident that wasn't an accident."

"And Tory, who was the intended victim of the accident, posed as her sister here, in Shelter Valley," Cassie said, remembering. "She took Christine's new job in the English department at Montford as a way to hide out."

"Right." Phyllis took a sip of tea. "She lived

with me before she met and married Ben. She thought I was doing all the helping in our relationship but she helped *me* realize that I was hating myself, blaming myself, for something the jerk I'd married had done. It wasn't my fault he was intimidated by me. It was his. There was nothing wrong with me. And plenty wrong with him. I was being a masochist, feeding my body stuff I didn't even want as a way to punish myself for not being woman enough to keep my man.''

Cassie couldn't believe how well Phyllis had just explained Cassie's own feelings of inadequacy. ''So what do I do?'' she asked softly. ''I don't have any weight to lose.''

''Search your heart,'' Phyllis said. ''Listen to what it tells you.''

''Sam wants us to try again, to find out if there's anything left of what we had.''

''Is that what you want?''

Cassie shook her head. She didn't need to listen to her heart. She already knew what it had to say. ''I can't trust him.'' *Or myself...*

''Maybe he had a reason for doing what he did. Something that would allow you to see things differently. Maybe the infidelity was a one-time thing. A horrible mistake.''

''It was that, all right,'' Cassie said, a trace of bitterness slipping through. ''But it wouldn't matter, even if there was some acceptable way to explain it.'' She rose to pour the rest of her tea down the sink and rinse her glass. "We can't ever go back to the life we'd planned. Things have changed for me, major things. Taking up where we left off is impossible.''

"Maybe you can create a new plan.''

Wiping her hands on the towel by the sink, Cassie thought about that. There was no new plan for her and Sam. Talking to Phyllis was only confirming that. "I can't forgive him.''

"And that's the basis of your problem,'' Phyllis said. "I don't blame you. I'm having a hard time in that area myself. But this I do know—you don't have to open your heart to him again, you don't have to trust him, but if you don't find a way to forgive him, you're never going to heal. You'll have allowed him to rob you not only of your past, but of your future, too.''

The words were hard to take. More so because Cassie knew that Phyllis was right. But forgiving was an agonizing business. It required thinking about things she'd promised herself she'd never think about again.

It required feeling things she was afraid to let herself feel.

IN HARMON'S HARDWARE store on Saturday afternoon—doing a bit of work while he waited for enough time to pass before he could go back to get

Mariah from the park—Sam perused a binder of
suppliers' information that Hank Harmon had just
given him.

He'd need everything, from nails and hammers
and wood glue to power tools and scaffolding. And
buying wholesale in bulk, at least for the supplies
he'd be replacing often, was much more cost-
effective than buying over the counter. No matter
how much money Sam had, he didn't believe in
wasting it. Not after the want he'd seen all over the
world.

"I suppose you've heard that Junior's trying to
pull the plug on Becca Parsons's Save the Youth
program," Hank said, an elbow on the counter,
watching Sam. His overalls looked as though he'd
worn them one day too many without washing.

"Mmm-hmm," Sam said, trying to focus on payment and delivery terms rather than the rock that
was taking form in his gut. Junior, as most people
dismissively called him, was the current mayor, and
derided for his lack of initiative and leadership. But
he was a Smith, the "other" branch of the Montfords. They'd been brought into the family by the
original Smith's marriage to the original Sam Montford's daughter. On the whole, the Smiths were
more self-centered than the Montfords, less civic-
minded and more mercenary. But they were of
Montford descent. And as the second-wealthiest
family in town, they had power in their own right.

Junior wasn't all bad. He wasn't evil, didn't have unethical business dealings. He just wasn't a doer. Or a thinker, either.

Now, Becca Parsons—that was another matter. Older than Sam by a decade, Becca was on the town council and married to the president of Montford University. No one loved Shelter Valley more than Becca did; no one served the town better.

"Your folks told you all about the play the youth program produced last summer, I'm sure." Hank tried again when it was obvious Sam wasn't going to bite. "It was the story of your great-great-grandfather's life."

"Yeah." Sam nodded. "I understand they performed it the day the statue was dedicated."

"That's right. It was great, too. Could rival anything you'd see in children's theater in Phoenix. And besides the theater division, the program's got a sports division, arts and crafts, drug and alcohol awareness, all kinds of things. They were planning to hold biweekly dances this summer, too, to let the kids get together in a controlled environment." Hank went on and on, as was his way, cheerfully imparting every bit of information he had. "The dances are one of Becca's newest projects. She wants to bring in DJs from Phoenix, do it up right so the kids'll not only want to come, but will feel like they can get everything in Shelter Valley that they'd get in the big city. She says it'll keep them from wandering, always thinking they have to run off to Phoenix for the real fun.''

Sam nodded a second time. He'd heard all about the project. Four times in the past week—though only once from his parents. He was in full support of it.

He just couldn't be responsible for it—or any of the other projects that were stalled or threatened by the spineless Junior Smith.

''You got a piece of paper, Hank?'' he asked, grabbing a pen from the counter.

With stained and callused fingers, Hank slid a pad of notepaper bearing the Harmon Hardware logo across the bottom toward him, and said, ''You know why Becca started the program, don't you?''

Sam nodded yet again, though he didn't look up from the names, numbers and figures he was copying. ''My folks had her and Will over for dinner last Monday night.''

It was the night after Sam had had his conversation with his parents about what his future plans did and did not entail. But to be fair, they'd already invited the Parsonses. It hadn't been a deliberate slap in Sam's face—or a refusal to accept the place he chose to occupy in Shelter Valley. Or more to the point, the place he chose *not* to occupy.

Regardless, he'd enjoyed renewing his acquaintance with Will and Becca. And he'd been charmed by little Bethany, who'd entertained them by rolling all over his mother's handwoven wool carpet.

"They tell you about Becca's niece being killed by that teenage drunk driver a couple years back?" Hank asked, his gaze intent.

Looking up from the page, Sam met Hank's eyes. "I think the program's great, Hank. I'm all for it."

With Mariah growing up in this town, he'd fight for that program, just as any other conscientious citizen would. He'd offer financial support, as well.

But that was all he could do.

"You know elections are coming up this next fall." Henry Crane, an optometrist who'd moved to Shelter Valley when Sam was just a kid, came up behind Sam. He'd obviously been eavesdropping.

The rock in Sam's stomach was getting bigger by the second. He owed this town; he knew that. He was a Montford—had been born to privilege. And responsibility.

But he had to pay in his own way. Didn't he?

Ron Christie, his ex-Little League baseball coach, now gray and walking with a cane, joined the threesome at the counter. "Yeah, and with you back in town, Sam..."

"Wait a minute, guys." Sam held up his hand. He couldn't let them go any further. "I'm a construction worker."

"You're a Montford," Chuck Taylor said. Chuck had been the quarterback of Sam's high-school football team. He'd gone on to play for Montford U, and then a couple of pro teams, before a knee injury forced his early retirement. Sam had heard that Chuck now owned a portion of the Shelter Valley Cactus Jelly Plant.

"Can't argue with you, there," Sam said, "I am a Montford." He tried to keep things light. Tried not to let the pressure of their hopes get to him.

The last time he'd done that—let the expectations of other people unsettle him—he'd made the biggest mistake of his life. He'd hightailed it to Phoenix. Gotten drunk. Slept with a woman whose name he couldn't remember. He'd betrayed Cassie. Run out on their marriage...

"What do you say," Chuck said. "You were always the guy leading the crusades."

Closing the binder, Sam slid it back across the counter to Hank. He turned to face the men—Chuck with his balding head and potbelly, Henry whose glasses had gotten much thicker over the years, and Ron who was far too skinny and frail for Sam's liking. He cared for them all. They represented what was best about Shelter Valley. Love. Loyalty. Home. You could count on all three of these guys for anything.

Sam hated to let any of them down.

"I appreciate your faith in me, gentlemen, but I don't even have a college degree. I'm not qualified to run this town."

Chuck lifted a booted foot up onto the barrel of electrical tape by the counter, leaning an elbow on his upraised knee. "Hell, Sam, you're the smartest guy I know. You could run this town in your sleep."

The thing was, there was probably truth in Chuck's assessment. While Sam might need to stay awake to sign checks, he *could* run Shelter Valley. He just didn't want to.

He'd promised himself before he came back here, that he wouldn't allow them to influence him. He would ignore their persuasions and compliments. At one time he couldn't handle the pressure this town put on him, and that had caused him to betray his wife, to hurt those he loved most, to destroy his life.

But he was stronger now. And armed with his hard-won self-knowledge, he wasn't going to fall into the trap of other people's desires.

On Monday, after work, Cassie went straight home, changed into an old pair of cut off shorts and a cropped T-shirt, and pulled her hair back into a ponytail. She had a mission.

She was going to tile the alcove in her guest bathroom.

Leaving on the television in her bedroom, she went to the kitchen, flipped on that set, and helped herself to a large glass of soda with lots of ice.

She'd eat later if she got hungry enough to quit work. Next stop was the garage for the supplies she'd bought the day before—the plastic floor protector, two-by-two, yellow-and-green ceramic tiles, paste and putty knife, and the hammer she was going to use to break the square shower tiles into smaller pieces.

She loved to decorate. Had studied interior decorating in the evenings a few years ago and still avidly read the magazines she received each month. After her talk with Phyllis, she'd decided to concentrate on something she loved, something other than her work. An activity that would take up her time, consume her.

With the set on in the bathroom, as well, she waited for her evening companions to appear and keep her company. She felt as though she knew Pat Sajak and Alex Trebek personally.

"Jeopardy" came on first. Cassie was on her knees cracking tile, angling the hammer to get varied shapes. Later she'd lay them out in designs that let the different colors and shapes complement each other, before applying them to the wall.

"What are Lisbon and Madrid?" she mumbled between cracks of the hammer. The two Iberian cities the Lusitania Express ran between.

As Diane, the thirty-something contestant with the stylish navy suit and short fly-away hair, asked the correct question, Cassie picked up the piece of tile she'd just broken. Round on one end, it was jagged on the other. She really liked that one. She set it aside to become a focal point in the finished design.

The television droned on. Tuning out the five minutes of commercials, Cassie continued to break up tiles, allowing her artistic eye freedom and refusing to let her mind roam. Sam had taken Mariah into Phoenix for an appointment with her counselor that afternoon. And he hadn't called with a report.

She didn't want to place too much importance on that.

Mariah hadn't made any more progress on Saturday. Had not, in fact, seemed as interested in Sammie. She hadn't looked at all while Cassie laughed and made a big production out of playing Frisbee with Zack's dog. And her little hand had merely rested on Sammie's head when Cassie brought the dog back to her. There was no burying of fingers in Sammie's fur.

But it could have been that she was simply taking comfort from the dog with less effort.

Or maybe she'd been paying more attention to Cassie. Cassie had been telling her about their senior prom, when she and Sam were crowned king and queen. She'd described the crown in great detail. And remembering back, she'd described Sam as she'd seen him that night. A true king—not just at the dance, but always.

"What is Nevada?" she said aloud. The show was back on. She had something to focus her thoughts on. The U.S. state that had sagebrush as its state flower.

She and Diane both got it right.

Diane chose "Feather Fun" for two hundred dollars. "The reptilian feature that evolved into feathers." Alex read.

"What are scales?" Cassie looked up, willing Diane, the person she was rooting for, to get it right. "Scales," she said again.

Before she found out if Diane knew the answer, the doorbell rang.

It was Sam.

"Where's Mariah?" she asked, opening the door, forgetting what she must look like. Forgetting she didn't want Sam there, alone with her, in her house. He was still wearing the slacks and polo shirt he must've worn for the trip in to Phoenix. His longish dark hair was mussed, his green eyes troubled. His face was grim.

"Home," he said, lips tight. "The trip into town tired her out. She fell asleep right after dinner."

"Your mother's with her?" Cassie asked. They didn't want Mariah waking up alone, being frightened, just when they'd begun to make a little progress.

Sam nodded. "I'm interrupting something?" he

asked, pointing to the hammer still clutched in her fist.

Glancing down at herself, Cassie brushed self-consciously at the tile dust on her knees. Though why it should matter what she looked like for this man, she didn't know. It didn't matter. Not at all. *He* didn't matter.

But his daughter did.

"I was just working in the guest bathroom," she explained.

He frowned. "Did you need help fixing something?"

Cassie shook her head. "I'm creating." Because his presence in her house was bothering her, making her too aware—uncomfortably aware—of her own confused feelings, she headed back to her project. She needed something other than Sam, other than her own emotions, to focus on.

Sam followed her, leaning against the sink as she showed him what she was doing. She felt like a nervous teenager.

"I'm impressed," he said, kneeling to put together a couple of odd-shaped pieces of tile. They complemented each other perfectly. "What kind of grout are you planning to use?"

Before she knew it, she and Sam were discussing the project in detail, with him giving construction pointers as she showed him her plans. Until that moment, she'd completely forgotten he was in the renovation business. That projects like this were the kind of work he did.

She found herself kneeling in her bathroom beside him, sharing ideas, approving of what she heard. Laughing at small jokes.

Almost like old friends.

Sam seemed more relaxed than when he'd first come in, and Cassie was glad. It was good to see the Sam she used to spend hours with, working on some project for school or planning a dinner party. He laughed, and her stomach melted.

When he reached over her for a piece of tile and his hand grazed her arm, Cassie stood up, moved away from him.

Things were suddenly far too intimate. Too dangerous.

"I imagine you had a reason for stopping by," she said, hammer in hand.

He placed a couple more tile shards in the mosaic they'd been building on the floor, brushed his hands and stood up.

The party was over.

"They want to institutionalize Mariah."

"No!" She took a step toward him, forgetting everything but the little girl who'd already grown to mean so much to her. "They can't *do* that to her! She shouldn't be with strangers, in a place where they're constantly testing her, monitoring her, studying her," Cassie said passionately. "She needs to be with family, with people who love her.''

"I know.''

"You're not going to let them do that, are you?'' she asked. "Jeopardy'' ended. "Wheel of Fortune'' came on, and Cassie didn't even notice.

Sam frowned. "I have to consider what's best for her. Her counselor believes that if putting her someplace where they can work with her every day, where they'll have several doctors assessing her, is going to help her—'' He broke off. "I don't know.''

"We're making progress, here, Sam. Taking her away from you now might just lock her away— emotionally—forever.'' Cassie might not have all the education that psychiatrist in Phoenix had, but she had a fair amount of training. Some relevant experience. And instincts that hadn't led her wrong yet.

"I know,'' Sam said. "Dr. Abrams mentioned that possibility. Cassie, she's already lost so much.''

The pain in his eyes broke through the ice that had to surround Cassie whenever she was with Sam. Making her heart bleed for him. For the decision he had to make.

And for the little girl whose future lay in the balance.

"What do your parents think?''

Sam shrugged, and she watched his solid shoulders move. He was leaning against the sink, facing her. And his back was reflected in the mirror behind him.

"They don't want to send her anywhere. At least, not yet," he said. "But we've lost six months of her life, Cassie. She's going to be a year behind in school if we can't get her back soon, help her catch up before next fall."

But to send that lonely, frightened little girl away? To an institution? No matter how they tried to fix those places up, they were still cold.

Because an institution wasn't home.

Cassie acknowledged that they were right for some people, with certain kinds of problems. But not Mariah.

The child would just die there. Or learn to cope—but in the process lose the person she really was. Both the love and the hatred in her past would be difficult to think about, painful to remember, but it had to happen if Mariah was to return to herself. And to them...

"She's in there, Sam," Cassie said urgently. "The fact that she watches you so intently has got to be a sign that you mean the world to her. If not, why doesn't she just stare at whatever happens to be around? It seems quite deliberate that she won't look at things—as though she's afraid to take them in, get too involved with her environment. But she takes *you* in. That has to mean something.''

The muscles in his jaw were working as he gazed at her, his eyes bright, emotions in check.

Cassie wanted so desperately to help him. *Needed* to help him. It was as if they were teenagers again, feeling each other's pain.

''Give me a little more time. I'll move more quickly, take her out of the park this week. Perhaps she'll participate more with the world if she's exposed to unfamiliar stimuli without you to focus on.''

''Sending her away seems so wrong,'' Sam said, the intense struggle he was experiencing evident in his voice. ''But what if I make a mistake? What if this *is* what she really needs? How can I rob her of that chance?''

Without conscious thought, Cassie reached out to Sam, grabbing his hand between both of hers so naturally that she didn't even notice what she'd done until the warmth of his skin sent shocks right through her. Abruptly, Cassie let go. ''Listen to your heart, Sam. It'll tell you what to do.''

Phyllis had given her the same advice a few days before. And recalling why, Cassie turned away.

''Cassie…'' He stretched out his hand, taking hers again.

Her skin burned, her body remembering other

times those fingers had touched her, and she found herself reacting automatically.

She jerked her hand away. "I'm here if you decide to continue," she said, turning from him. "Just let me know."

"Cassie," he said again.

Cassie didn't face him. She couldn't. She faced the bathtub, instead, and listened to Pat Sajak congratulate a winner as he started the next round.

Sam didn't try to talk to her any more, but he was taking a long time leaving. She didn't know how much more she could stand.

"Can you still do tomorrow afternoon?" His voice sounded weary when he eventually spoke.

"Of course." Cassie looked over her shoulder at him, but only briefly. "We can meet in the park as usual." *Go now,* she silently begged.

"Thanks," he said, and it sounded as if he'd turned to go.

Cassie waited.

"And thanks for listening," he added. "You have no idea how badly I needed to see you tonight...."

She waited until she heard the front door click quietly behind him before she turned around.

And then, with her three televisions droning in the background, she fell to the floor, buried her face in the tile dust and sobbed until her ribs ached.

CHAPTER ELEVEN

THINGS AT BOROUGH BANTAM were running amuck. The king and queen had adopted a little mouse that had crawled into their town. They were preoccupied, scurrying around, trying to please the little creature. Their usual pursuits were being neglected.

Leaning over his desk, Sam concentrated on the page coming to life beneath his rapidly moving pencil. Without the king and queen's watchful eye, the kingdom was falling into chaos and disrepair, and the magistrate was too busy worming around his empty little circle to see anything wrong. *I am. I am. I am.*

Without forethought, Sam moved to the last frame of this week's episode, a figure of the newcomer—the wild stallion—forming quite naturally. He was sitting under a ledge, gnawing on a piece of straw, a cowboy hat on his head while he watched. And waited.

The king and queen glanced at him from time to time. They weren't opposed to his being there. But they were withholding judgment.

Could be that they were too involved with their new addition to give him their complete attention. Or that he'd never be fully welcome here.

So, did he have a role in Borough Bantam? A purpose? Or was this just a stopping place on his way somewhere else?

Eager to find out, Sam was looking forward to next week's episode.

"PHYLLIS? IT'S CASSIE. Am I interrupting something?"

"I'm grading papers, so interrupt away."

Cassie grinned. It'd been so long since she'd allowed herself friends. "I have a question for you."

"What's up?"

"Sam came by last night and said that Mariah's doctor in Phoenix has suggested the possibility of institutionalizing her. Sam doesn't want to do it. And I don't think he should." Cassie glanced at the television playing softly in the background in her office. "At least, not yet. We're making progress with Sammie. We just need a little more time."

"Reaching her in a normal life environment, if it's possible, is certainly better than trying to do it in the controlled environment of a hospital," Phyllis said slowly, as though choosing her words carefully.

"Then you think I was right to encourage Sam not to rush into anything?"

"As long as he's comfortable with continuing the way you are."

"He says his instincts are telling him to hang on to her."

"Then he probably should."

"That's what I thought, too."

"They *might* get quicker results in an institution. Forcing her to respond within a very predictable, structured situation, having her live around other traumatized kids, surrounded by caring staff—it could work," Phyllis said. "But not necessarily. And not necessarily with the best results."

"What do you mean by that?" Cassie had another fifteen minutes before her first appointment of the day. And she'd been worrying about Sam and Mariah for most of the night.

"Just that Mariah might come out of herself a little sooner that way, but she may not emerge as completely."

"She might be emotionally alienated," Cassie said. "Disaffected. Able to function adequately on a surface, everyday level but lacking emotional depth."

"Right." Phyllis gave Cassie a rundown of several cases in which recovery had been complete after the patient had been allowed to recuperate from a tragedy in her own time, in the safe environment of a loving home. "It takes longer sometimes, but the result could be a perfectly normal, well-adjusted life.''

''Rather than one with dysfunctional relationships due to an inability to feel, to open oneself to others.''

Thinking of the little girl who'd stolen her heart, a heart that had been empty since she'd lost her own little girl, Cassie knew which scenario she'd rather have. It was up to her and Sammie to make sure Mariah got that chance.

SAM, DRESSED IN CUTOFFS and an equally revealing tank top, brought Mariah to the park right on time the next afternoon. Cassie's breath caught in her throat. He was so gorgeous.

A couple of mothers with strollers watched him cross the park. Sam seemed completely oblivious.

Cassie wished *she* was oblivious to *him*.

How was it possible, after all he'd done, that she could still feel such attraction?

The women followed him with their eyes, one leaning toward the other to say something. They both nodded; the second woman said something. They both laughed.

Probably fantasizing, Cassie thought. About how good that body would look stepping out of the shower, slick and wet. The chest would be contoured to perfection, firm to a woman's touch. The hair would be dripping over his forehead and into his eyes, large drops of clear, warm water...

He strode with such confidence, yet was the epitome of tenderness as he leaned toward his daughter, giving the unresponsive child his entire attention. He spoke to her as though they were both involved in the conversation.

The woman across the park actually turned around to stare once he'd left their line of vision. His tight backside wouldn't disappoint them.

Cassie could practically see them drooling.

He's mine, she wanted to tell those women. *He's always been mine.*

But the moment wasn't real. It was like a scene from a movie she was watching. Or a particularly good book she was reading to pass the time on this warm April afternoon. She was just a witness. It wasn't happening to her.

Until Sam and Mariah reached her and Cassie couldn't find the breath to say hello.

Oh, God. What was happening to her? She was losing control of her world.

Sammie greeted Mariah, butting her head up under the little girl's free hand.

"Is an hour long enough?" Sam asked, looking at her strangely.

Cassie nodded.

"Right here?"

"Yeah." She found her voice. And hoped her composure wasn't far behind.

He lowered himself to Mariah's eye level as he let go of her hand. "You stay with Cassie and Sammie, okay, honey?" he said. "Daddy has some work to do in town, and then I'll be right back to get you."

Mariah stared at him, making no response, her little face lifting as he rose.

Good luck, Sam mouthed to Cassie. With one last, concerned look in her direction, he turned his back and walked away.

As intent as Mariah, Cassie stared after him until he was out of sight. Something would have to give soon. Before Cassie's sanity did.

Maybe it was time to go to Phoenix and find herself a man. But after ten years of celibacy, she wasn't sure she'd know what to do with one if she had him.

She couldn't imagine *wanting* one. Not if he wasn't Sam.

And she didn't want Sam at all.

CASSIE DECIDED to take Mariah to the ice-cream shop. Close to the park, the shop was fairly safe, she thought, since she could get the child back to her usual spot if it appeared that the outing was going to upset her too much. And all kids loved ice cream. Didn't they?

"You like chocolate ice cream?" Cassie asked the little girl, as soon as Sam had been gone long enough for her heart to slow down to its normal speed.

Mariah didn't answer. Nor did she react when Cassie took the small hand Sam had dropped. Mariah didn't pull back, and she didn't grab hold. The limp little fingers just lay in Cassie's grasp.

"Have you been to the Shelter Valley ice-cream shop yet?" Cassie asked, starting down the sidewalk as though there was no doubt that Mariah would walk beside her. "Come on, Sammie."

As Sammie moved, so did Mariah, although the little girl looked neither left nor right. Or straight in front of her, for that matter. Her stare was almost vacant, focused—if you could call it that—on some point between her waist and the ground.

Cassie refused to be daunted; the possibility that Mariah might be placed in an institution kept her going. She chatted all the way to the ice-cream shop, trying to engage Mariah's interest. The child had a difficult moment when she had to leave Sammie to wait outside as they reached the door, but when Cassie turned and walked inside, Mariah followed, her hand sliding from the dog's head.

Cassie ordered them each a scoop of ice cream in a paper cup. "You'll have to hold this one, honey, until we get outside." When Mariah made no move to accept it, Cassie lifted the child's hand, placed her fingers around the cup, then carefully let go. Mariah held on to the cup.

Without another word, Cassie took Mariah's free hand and ushered the child outside and back to Sammie.

Sammie started off walking at Cassie's side, between her and the street, and Mariah did an amazing thing. She dropped Cassie's hand and switched to the other side, between Cassie and Sammie. She couldn't touch the dog, not if she was holding Cassie's hand and a cup of ice cream, too. But she'd made her point. She and Sammie stuck together.

Cassie blinked back tears as she silently applauded the little girl.

ZACK DIDN'T WANT to do it, but Randi made him. She and Ben had set up a little game of basketball at the university on Friday afternoon, making use of the vacant gym, and Randi thought he should call Sam and invite him to join them.

Zack, who saw no point in encouraging the man to hang around, argued with her until she reminded him he could bring Sammie, Sam could bring Mariah, and the two could have a little session of pet therapy without involving Cassie.

That was incentive enough. He'd seen Cassie through the worst of times, but he'd never seen her quite the way she'd been this past week. Focused and determined one minute; lost the next.

Keeping her away from Sam, even for one session, was a good enough reason to ruin a game he'd been looking forward to. Though, he had to admit, he was a little surprised by how readily Sam agreed to join them. Either the man was stupid—Zack's personal opinion—or he didn't care that he'd be hanging out with people who came pretty close to hating him.

When Ben heard that Mariah was coming, he decided to bring Alex along, as well, giving Tory a few hours to herself to catch up on the study time she'd missed the night before, when she'd had to comfort a crying Alex and rock her to sleep. The girl's natural mother had called that day, catching Alex before Tory or Ben knew who was on the phone, and had brought back memories that were still recent enough to disturb the child.

Ben had told Zack this morning that Alex's mother wanted him not to testify in the child abuse trial Alex's natural father was facing. Ben refused to consider such an option. He expected to be subpoenaed but even he wasn't, he intended to represent his daughter's interests. Zack couldn't help wondering if it might be best to let it go and get that white trash out of Alex's life, once and for all.

But that was a conversation he'd have with his friend on another day.

Zack had been watching from center court as Sam arrived with his daughter; the other man immediately spotted Sammie and walked Mariah over to her.

"You sit right here, honey."

Zack's heart lurched when, without taking her eyes from her father, Mariah sat down, inched as close to Sammie as she could, and laid her hand on the dog's head.

Damn. Cassie was right. Sam's little girl could be reached. At least, by Zack's dog.

She was right about something else, too. Sam Montford was devoted to his adopted daughter; the look on his face made that abundantly clear.

But as far as Zack was concerned, the man still had a lot to answer for.

"So, we doing two on two?" Randi asked, as soon as Ben had joined them on the court.

Zack sized up his three opponents. Ben and Sam, both dressed in gym shorts and tank-style T-shirts, had a lot of muscle. Zack knew he could take Ben at least half the time. Which left Sam the unknown entity.

"Since I want a friendly bed-partner tonight, I'm not playing against you, Zachary," Randi said, grinning. She looked at Sam and Ben. "He hates it when I win."

"Because you cheat," Zack said, grinning back at her.

"I do not." Her chin jutted out sexily. "It's merely a case of brain over brawn."

She was going to pay for her sassiness when he got her home—probably even before dinner—and she knew it. That was why she egged him on. They both loved the payback.

"Brain, my a—"

"Zack!" Randi said, as the men laughed. "There are children present."

"Yeah, Zack, I'm present!" Alex called from the corner of the gym. She was sitting on Sammie's other side, coloring.

"Did you ask Mariah if she wanted to color, squirt?" Ben asked.

"Yeah, but I don't think she does."

Randi bounced the basketball at her feet. "Okay, Sam and Ben against me and Zack. Jump ball!"

She waited while Zack and Sam got into position, then tossed the ball up.

Zack came down with the ball. Barely. And he had the most uncomfortable feeling that Sam had let him have it.

The game was grueling, but Zack had to admit that it felt damn good to pound Sam Montford on the basketball court. Or at least to attempt it. He was on the man full court, never letting up. Trying to steal the ball every time Sam had possession, blocking every shot or pass he tried to make.

The score reflected his aggression. But not as much as he would've expected. He and Randi were barely ahead. Not only that, but Randi seemed a little annoyed when she met Zack under their basket about ten minutes into the game. Sam and Ben were in-bounding the ball.

"Cool it," she wheezed, slightly out of breath.

Zack glanced down at her, loving her so much it hurt. "I can't," he said simply. The cousins made their way down the court. "He deserves it."

Zack couldn't wait for her reply; he ran up-court, guarding Sam.

With some impressive footwork, Sam got around him and scored. Zack moved to the sideline to take the ball that Randi was going to throw him.

"I know he deserves it," she whispered, pretending to talk strategy with him. "But you're a better man than this. And he's getting his come-uppance. He's not happy. My guess is he's still in love with Cassie. What better punishment than to live this close to her, see her all the time, and know he can never have her?"

Imagining himself living in the same town as Randi without the right to take her home to bed every night, to wake beside her every morning, to listen to her fears and laugh at her jokes, Zack agreed with her. Sam Montford was getting the punishment he truly deserved.

He just hoped Cassie didn't end up suffering, too. She was the sister he'd never had, and Zack was going to protect her. Come hell or high water.

A little while later, Ben said he needed some

water. Sam was looking a little thirsty himself. But Zack wasn't finished with him.

Zack didn't have any choice. The other three walked off the court and left him standing there. Sam and Ben saw to their daughters, showing them to the bathroom, then Ben gave both of them juice boxes from Alex's miniature backpack. Afterward, the two men retrieved water bottles from the bags they'd brought with them and stood at the end of the court, dripping sweat and squirting water into their mouths.

Randi had disappeared into her office for something. Zack stood off to the side, figuring he'd much rather be in Randi's office with her than on the court with these two. Even though Ben was just about the best friend he'd ever had.

"So what're you studying at the university?" Sam asked Ben, as they leaned against the gym wall. Sam was watching Mariah, who hadn't touched the box of juice Ben had placed on the floor in front of her. Zack wasn't even sure she knew it was there. She'd been staring at Sam the entire game, her little head moving back and forth as Sam ran up and down the court.

But her eyes, as far as Zack had been able to tell, had not followed the play at all. They'd only followed Sam.

"I'm starting out with a business degree." Ben

was answering Sam. "I thought about law, but that'll have to wait a while."

"Ben's spent the past eight years supporting Alex and her mother so he's getting a late start on his education," Zack chimed in. "But he's carrying a 4.0. As soon as he graduates, there'll be no stopping him."

Zack rather enjoyed bragging about Sam's cousin's accomplishments in the face of Sam's failures.

"Business, huh?" Sam asked, eyes narrowing as he took them off Mariah long enough to look at Ben. "Life at a desk appeals to you?"

Ben shrugged. "Don't know about that. Manipulating money appeals to me. Especially when I'm manipulating it in my direction." He grinned an all-male grin.

Sam, doing a damn fine job of dividing his attention between his daughter and the conversation at hand, smiled at Mariah. At the same time he asked Ben, "You working now?"

Ben shook his head. "I saved enough to get through this first year. It's been so long since I was in school, I wasn't sure what I was signing on for, but I'm going to look for something this summer." He glanced over at Alex. "To be honest, I didn't count on supporting a wife and daughter, when I made my plans."

"Have you talked to my father?" Sam asked. "You're entitled to Montford money."

Silently sipping his own bottle of water, Zack searched for the malice, the jealousy or selfishness behind Sam's offer. Even a little bitterness would have been a welcome confirmation of his opinion. He wasn't all that happy when he heard none of them. He didn't want to find anything impressive about the man who'd damn near destroyed one of his dearest friends.

Ben pushed away from the wall, tossing his empty water bottle in the big plastic can at the end of the court. "I don't take handouts," he said. "When I'm rich, it's going to be because I made myself that way through honest hard work."

Sam jogged onto the court beside Ben. Zack followed, but hung back just a little, waiting for Randi.

"There's a job available at Montford, Inc., if you're interested," Sam said, grabbing the ball from Ben to make a hook shot. "But I gotta tell you, if you take it, you might have to be mayor of Shelter Valley someday, too. It all comes with the Montford territory."

Sam made the job sound like a death sentence.

And if he felt that way about it, Zack wondered, how had he handled growing up in this town, where half the people still thought he was their savior come back to rescue them. That would've been one hell of a lot of pressure for a young guy.

It gave Zack an insight into the man, one he wasn't ready to accept. He was on Cassie's side. That meant he needed to hate Sam Montford, not sympathize with him.

THEY WERE ALL TIRED, but too damn stubborn to quit without a win, when a couple of Montford's senior basketball players came barreling into the gym for a little one on one. Zack recognized them immediately. At the U on scholarship, both men were destined for the pros as soon as they graduated the following month. They'd both already signed with well-known agents.

"Hey, Bo, Glen," Randi called out to them. "Come to let us old folks show you how it's done?"

"Hell no, Coach," Bo called back across the court, whipping a basketball at Randi's middle. "Come to give you few lessons."

The boys made a couple of spirited runs up and down the court with the four of them, everyone enjoying a healthy bout of physical competition. No one noticed the little girl sitting on the sidelines, her hand gripping the dog crouched next to her.

Not until Bo got a little too rough with Sam, knocking him flat when Sam came down with a rebound. Sam was still on the floor, his nose dripping blood, when Sammie's pain-filled yelp resounded through the gym, deafening them all, turning seven pairs of alarmed eyes in her direction. Mariah was shaking so hard that she was almost convulsing, her eyes unfocused as she stared vacantly somewhere in the distance. In her little hand was a hank of Sammie's fur. Pulled from the dog's neck.

"Oh, my God!" Zack heard Randi's cry, as he and Sam raced to the little girl's side. Running, Sam wiped his nose on a towel Glen had thrown him.

"Mariah?" His voice was filled with love. And overflowing with fear. "What's wrong, honey? Daddy's right here." He dabbed at his nose again.

Even though he'd been down on the floor, he reached her first, lifting her gently into his arms, cradling her against him.

"Daddy's right here, honey," he said, over and over, attempting to calm the child.

Zack had never seen such terror in another man's eyes, as the little girl continued to shake.

"She's scared to death," Sam said.

"Sammie's just fine, honey," Zack said, with no idea what to do. "She just makes noises like that sometimes. It's nothing to be afraid of."

His eyes met Sam's. Something more than the dog's yelp had done this. Something that had made Mariah react convulsively, yanking out Sammie's fur. "Randi's gone for her blood pressure cuff. Should I have her call an ambulance?"

"I don't know," Sam said. "I'm afraid having strangers fussing over her would only scare her more." He rubbed the little girl's back, tried to see the face she had hidden in his chest. "What do you think?"

Ben, with Alex in his arms, came up behind them. "Is there anything I can do?"

Sam shook his head. "Why don't you take Alex home?" he suggested. The other little girl looked scared to death.

"You'll call me later, let me know she's okay?" Ben asked anxiously.

Nodding, Sam turned his attention back to his daughter, trying to persuade her to release him long enough for him to see her face, to assess the situation.

The two boys, after making sure there was nothing they could do, had disappeared, leaving Zack and Sam alone in the gym with Mariah.

"Should we call her doctor?" Zack asked. He'd never felt so helpless in his life. Never seen another man look that way.

Mariah was still shaking.

"I've got her psychiatrist's number in my wallet over in my bag. Would you mind?" Sam asked.

Without another word, Zack ran off, grabbed Sam's wallet, and was at a phone by the time he'd found the number.

One thing was certain. Sam Montford's love for his daughter was very real and as deep as it gets. And no man who cared that much for a child who wasn't even his own could be all bad.

CHAPTER TWELVE

AN OLD ANDY GRIFFITH rerun was on after the late news on Friday night. It was the one in which a very young Opie was in love with Barney Fyfe's girl, Thelma Lou. Cassie had seen it often enough that she didn't need to look at the screen to know what was happening as she listened. And grouted.

All the tile was now applied to the wall. It had dried sufficiently that she could smear the grout on. And then begin the painstaking job of rubbing off the excess. It was a lot of work, but she was going to be very happy with the result. The guest bath might turn out to be her best room yet.

This time, when her doorbell rang, she knew instinctively who it was. She'd been letting the machine get the phone all night, as Zack was on call at the clinic and she was elbow-deep in sticky white stuff.

Not that Sam should be calling *or* visiting her. They'd already confirmed her Saturday-afternoon session with Mariah.

Wiping her hands on the towel slung over her shoulder, Cassie made her way slowly toward the front door. Wearing the same cutoffs and T-shirt she'd had on the night before, she wasn't even wearing a bra. She was barefoot and had tied her hair back with an elastic. She was not prepared to receive anyone. Especially not her ex-husband.

Sam was getting into the very bad habit of stopping by unannounced. She was going to have to cure him of that.

The bell pealed a second time.

"I'm coming," Cassie called. Whatever he wanted, he was just going to have to tell her while they stood on her front porch. He wasn't coming in her house again.

Flicking on the porch light, she pulled open the door.

Sam's face was ashen, his lips tight. The blood drained from Cassie's cheeks as she stepped back, allowing him room to come in. "What's wrong?"

"Mariah had an attack today."

"An attack?" Cassie asked, frowning, following him into her living room. He looked freshly showered, was wearing a pair of khaki shorts and a black polo shirt with black sandals. "What kind of attack? Where? When?"

"We were playing basketball," Sam said, shaking his head. "Zack and Randi, Ben and I. Mariah was sitting on the side of the court with Sammie and Alex, staring as usual. I never noticed anything amiss."

Cassie slid down beside him on the couch, her fingers itching to hold his hand, to smooth the still-damp tendrils of hair back from his eyes. She knew so naturally how to comfort him.

"Suddenly Sammie lets out this horrendous yelp, and Mariah's practically convulsing."

Oh, God. This was bad. "She had a seizure?" Did that mean there was brain damage, after all?

"No, thank God." He shook his head, his shoulders slumped forward, hands between his knees. "She was severely traumatized by something and couldn't seem to stop shaking."

"Where is she now?" They hadn't institutionalized her, had they? Not that quickly.

"Home. She's been given a sedative. She'll be out the rest of the night."

Home. Cassie started to breathe again.. "You've seen her psychiatrist, then?"

"No." He looked over at her, his green eyes filled with agony. And doubt. "I spoke to her briefly this afternoon. She had me go to the urgent-care clinic here in town to make sure there wasn't anything physically wrong."

"Which there isn't."

"Right."

Cassie's relief was tangible and so overwhelming, she forgot she had to draw a circle around herself to keep Sam out.

"We have an appointment with the psychiatrist on Monday." His eyes were clouded.

"You're thinking they might want to keep her."

"Her doctor said as much."

"Shit."

He shook his head, glanced over his shoulder at her. "Maybe it's for the best, Cassie. Maybe this is what she needs."

"Do you truly think so?"

"No." His expression was fierce. Then he looked away, his hands clasped. "But what do I know?"

"You know that you love her, that you'll do whatever it takes to help her."

"Which certainly doesn't qualify me to make this decision."

"I think," Cassie said slowly, "that perhaps, when it comes to parenting, you're supposed to trust your instincts."

She was actually sitting there, advising Sam on how to be a good parent. She, who could never be one herself. At some point, this memory was going to hurt.

"Doctors aren't always right, Sam."

His mouth a grim line, Sam didn't look convinced.

"At least, promise me you'll get a second opinion before you do anything."

"She's already with the best doctors available."

Her head shot up, her eyes searching his face. "So, you're just going to send her away?"

"No." He shook his head. "How can I desert her like that?"

He couldn't. She'd known that.

"But I'm not sure I'm making the decision that's best for Mariah," he added. "Maybe, because of my own need to keep her close, I'm merely deferring the inevitable."

"I've seen some miraculous things over the past couple of years, Sam—things that even the best psychologists in the nation didn't expect. I don't think you're wrong to give her this chance. The hospital will always be there."

He nodded. "She's already lost six months. It seems like an awfully long time to lose...."

Not compared to a lifetime. Cassie swallowed. Their own daughter had lost a lifetime. Sometime, she'd have to tell him about that.

But not now. She wasn't strong enough to get through that. Not yet. Not until she could trust herself to talk about her baby girl and remain immune to her baby's father.

"These past six months haven't been lost," Cassie finally said. "You've been loving that little girl, building a new sense of security for her, a new life, that will be there for her when she's ready to come out of hiding. I'm not pushing this because of the pet therapy, Sam. I don't have an agenda, and I don't need another test case. It's just that I've seen situations like this before. The slow building of trust. The successes. I know we're reaching her...."

Sam's eyes filled with worry. And hope.

Mariah was luckier then she knew. Cassie would've given anything to have Sam's steady, gentle caring during the months after their baby had died. To have the security of his love, while she came to grips with the fact that she wasn't ever going to have other children.

"Mariah's got a better chance with you, Sam." She couldn't fight for the daughter she'd lost, but she could fight for this child who'd lost her parents. "I really believe that withdrawing your constant love and support right now could interfere with her ability to become emotionally whole."

"You really care, don't you," he asked softly.

"Of course I care. I've spent a lot of time with that kid. She's a special little girl." It couldn't be any more than that.

He turned to face her. "And do you exact promises concerning the welfare of all your patients?"

Cassie held his gaze as long as she could. And then looked down. "I care about them all," she prevaricated. "I couldn't expend so much emotional energy on them *without* caring."

He watched her silently, and Cassie brushed at some tile dust on her knee. Fiddled with a strand of hair that had come loose.

"Do you ever wear it down anymore?"

The soft question took her by surprise. "Not usually. It gets in the way when I'm working."

"Pity."

He'd always loved her hair. Had often begged her never to cut it. That thought had come to mind a couple of times over the years when she'd been tempted just to chop off the whole fiery mess.

"So you don't have any idea what set Mariah off?" Cassie asked, squeezing her hands between her knees.

"Not for sure." Sam's expression lost the intensely personal look. "We weren't doing anything any different than we'd been doing for the hour or so we'd been playing."

"You said Sammie yelped. She didn't do anything to frighten Mariah, did she?" Cassie could hardly imagine such a thing. Sammie was too smart, too well-trained, to slip up. Cassie was convinced the dog cared for her charges as much as Cassie did.

"She yelped because Mariah had just yanked out a fistful of her fur."

Cassie frowned. "So something upset her *before* Sammie made any noise."

Leaning his elbows on his knees, Sam said, "Obviously."

"And you noticed nothing different in the room?"

"Nope." He frowned slightly as he apparently tried to picture the gym in the moments before Sammie yelped. "I'd just gone up for a rebound and landed on the floor, but it wasn't the first time that happened."

Cassie's mind raced. There had to be something there. Something that might help them understand what Mariah was hiding behind those beautiful blue eyes. "Maybe she thought you were hurt."

"Actually, my nose was bleeding a little," he said. "Do you think, considering what she saw the day her parents died…?"

"It *has* to be connected, Sam," Cassie insisted. "And if we know that much, we can help her. She reacted because she was remembering and—"

"What if we're wrong, Cass?" He voiced his darkest fear. "What if I decide to keep her with me and she never gets better?"

"The same could happen if you send her away."

Her tone reminded him they'd been through all that. But Sam just couldn't seem to shake the feeling that he was going to let Mariah down somehow.

"Now tell me again about the game," Cassie continued. "Zack was guarding you, you said."

"Like a killer whale on a hunk of meat."

"So he was the one who knocked you down?"

"No." Sam shook his head. "A couple of basketball players had joined us by that point, and I think it was one of them who caught me on the way down from the rebound.''

Cassie sat up straighter. It took everything Sam had not to pull her up against him. Her warmth would do so much to dissipate the cold that had infiltrated his body.

"I thought you said it was just the four of you."

He shrugged. "It was, right up until the last few minutes when a couple of guys joined us.''

"Who were the guys? What did they look like?''

Sam threw up his hands, let them fall again. "I don't know. They were a couple of students, Cassie. There was nothing harmful about them, if that's what you're thinking.''

She frowned. "I don't know what I'm thinking, but it seems more than coincidence that she was fine right up until the end. And it was only then that the boys were there.''

Wishing he could smooth that frown from her brow, Sam said, "They did nothing to her. I don't even think they noticed her.''

"What did they look like?''

"I don't know, not threatening." Sam tried to remember them, but since Mariah's bout, the rest of the afternoon had become a blur to him. "They were pretty tall, I guess. One of them skinnier than the other, but neither one was all that big.'' He shook his head again. "I'd never seen them before.''

A spark lit Cassie's eye. "They were strangers. And in her view, they attacked you. They hurt you, made your nose bleed."

"You may be right," he said thoughtfully. "The way Zack had been guarding me, it was the first time anyone else got close." He glanced at Cassie. "And there was blood on my face."

Cassie leaned forward, touching Sam's hand. "That has to be it. She saw the blood. And didn't you say she watched the terrorists hit her father?"

"You really think she was remembering?"

"I'm almost certain of it."

"So she hasn't blocked the horror," Sam said aloud, feeling sick. "She's living with it, day in and day out."

"Who's to say?" Cassie asked, leaving her hand on top of his. "Maybe she was blocking it until today, and now it's all going to come back to her. Maybe she *needs* to remember in order to heal."

"Maybe."

He stared at her. "Do you really think that's it?"

"It's possible, Sam." Cassie's look was sympathetic. "But it's just as possible that she's been remembering all along, torturing herself for some reason. Until she can talk to us, we just won't know."

As Sam digested her words, anger, frustration and hopeless despair built inside him. He was solely responsible for another human life, a little girl who was struggling and hurt, and there didn't seem to be a damn thing he could do to help her. What was it with him? Why did he always let down the people he loved?

"Hey." Cassie's hand traveled up his arm and back again, grabbing his right hand. "She's going to be okay. I really believe that."

Sam covered her hand with his left. With the exception of the one time he'd done something so reprehensible that he'd had to cut himself off from her, Cassie had always been able to rescue him from the darkness. From the void fashioned within his own mind.

He'd never needed rescuing more than he did that night.

"It's just going to take time. And a lot of love," Cassie continued through his silence. "We'll reach her, Sam. I know we will."

He tried to smile, but his jaw was too tight; he squeezed her hand again, instead. He had so many questions and not a single answer. No set course. No right way. He'd never felt so lost.

They sat together, connected, silent, for several minutes. Cassie's warmth seeped into him, reminding him so vividly of how it used to be for them. Every disappointment, every worry, had been diminished by their sharing. With Cassie he'd been completely unguarded. With her he'd felt safe. Until it all started closing in on him...

Sam didn't know when his hold on her changed

from seeking comfort to seeking more. The decision was not a conscious one, but rather a progression that was so natural he didn't even see it coming. One minute he was holding her hand, and the next he was caressing the underside of it.

Rather than fighting him, as an hour ago he'd have predicted she would, Cassie leaned into Sam, resting her head on his shoulder. And suddenly it dawned on him that he might not be the only one in need of rescuing.

His strong, valiant, beautiful ex-wife was fighting battles, too. Was she searching for a way out of her private agonies? Just like he was?

Peering around him at her attractive, well-ordered house, at the furnishings that looked as if they were straight out of a decorating magazine, Sam had a tough time matching Cassie's surroundings with the vivacious young woman he'd known her to be.

Where was that woman? Behind the career she seemed to live by? Underneath the showcase rooms? Hidden by the television shows that were so much a part of her life?

Could Sam help her find her way out?

Once, he would've been sure of it. "Cass?"

"Shh." She slowly moved her head against his arm as if saying no. But she didn't back away.

He pulled her hand between both of his. Her fingers were cold. "Are you okay?"

"Just give me a minute."

Glancing down, all he could see was the top of her head. Because, after ten years away from her, he wasn't sure what she needed, he did the only thing he could. He listened to his instincts.

His arm stole around her shoulders, and he settled her against his chest, in a position so natural to them, it was as though they'd never been separated. Still holding her hand, he brought it close to his body, running two fingers up and down her forearm.

The minute she showed any resistance, he'd let her go. But if she needed this connection—this intimacy—anywhere near as badly as he did, there was no way he could deny her.

"Remember the night Jamie Littleton died?" he asked a few moments later.

"Yeah."

It had been terrible for both of them. Jamie was the youngest son of some friends of Sam's parents'. The two of them had baby-sat Jamie practically since he was born. As teenagers, they'd pretended a time or two that Jamie's house was their own, that he was their son, that they were raising him together. They'd been practicing for the day they both knew was coming, when they really would have a home and children of their own.

And then one morning Jamie's mother had called

to say she'd just come from the doctor. Jamie had leukemia.

The day he'd died had been the darkest either Sam or Cassie had ever known. It had been their first experience with life's harder realities. The fragility of it all. Their first realization that they weren't invincible. That there were things they couldn't control. Things they couldn't prevent, no matter how zealous they were.

Over the two years of Jamie's illness, they'd managed to raise a lot of money for the leukemia foundation. They just hadn't managed to save Jamie's life.

"I was feeling pretty hopeless the night he died, and scared to death," Sam admitted, remembering back. "And then you came over...."

"You held me, just like this."

"And, although I was still just as sad, I felt so much better..."

"...like even though there were horrible things in life, there'd always be good things to help you through."

Sam had other memories of that night. Some of the most beautiful memories. "We made love for the first time...."

Cassie was silent, but he knew she was remembering, too. Her palm was still against his stomach, her fingers moving lightly against his shirt.

There was so much more he needed to say to

her, to explain. He needed her to know how much he'd loved her that night. He needed her to know that the feeling had never stopped.

"Is it too late for us, Cass?" he whispered, tilting her face up to his. "Does it have to be too late?"

He couldn't read the expression in her eyes as clearly as he'd once been able to. She'd learned how to hide her thoughts. Or perhaps they weren't clear even to her.

She didn't answer him, just continued to look up at him, pleading.

"What?" he asked. "What can I do to make you happy again?"

Her lips trembling, she opened her mouth, but didn't say anything.

"I'll do anything to make you happy again," he whispered, knowing in his heart that even if it meant leaving her forever, he would do so. His years away had taught him the value of what Cassie had once given him so openly.

Tears sprang to her eyes and she tried to blink them away. They spilled down her cheeks, and Sam lowered his head, gently kissing her face, kissing away her tears.

Cassie's moan was filled with need. With regret. And pain.

Sam's body throbbed, responding automatically to the cry it recognized. Her head turned, and her lips met his in a kiss that stopped his world from spinning so crazily out of control.

And spun *him* out of control, instead.

She tasted so perfectly right. So familiar. And so, so hungry. Hardening instantly, Sam welcomed her kiss. "Cass, are you sure?" he asked throatily, barely able to get the words past his own hunger.

"Don't talk, Sam," she begged. "Please, don't talk. Just love me."

He wanted to talk. He needed to know that being there, doing this, was as right for her as it was for him. He'd told her he thought they had a second chance.

Had she decided they did, too?

Her hands, roaming freely over his body, were telling him with unmistakable clarity what she wanted. Her words had told him the same thing. Sam could deny her nothing.

With a heavy groan, he rolled her over, down to the floor, and kissed her as he'd never kissed her before. Like a mature man kisses the woman he loves.

For the first time in ten years, his life felt right again.

CHAPTER THIRTEEN

CASSIE COULDN'T SLOW DOWN. Couldn't slow her rapidly beating heart, her panting, the blood racing through her veins or the heat burning in her belly. Her body was trembling, groping. She'd been starved for so long.

She was strong. Had been strong all these years, battling emotions that threatened to overwhelm her. And Sam's familiar hands holding her, his lips on hers, felt—right.

It was so long since she'd been touched. Forever. A lifetime ago.

"You are beautiful," Sam whispered against her neck. His lips trailed downward, leaving little kisses in their wake. Along her neck, pushing against the ribbed top of her T-shirt to reach her collarbone.

He pulled the elastic out of her hair, spreading the long strands around her.

"Mmm." Cassie hardly recognized the sounds she was making. She wasn't herself. Wasn't in control. No thought. No conscience. Just instinct.

She explored Sam's body eagerly, the solid masculine shoulders a delight. And so much larger than she remembered. His ears were the same as she recalled them, though. Cassie's tongue flicked across the lobe. He liked that. He'd always liked that.

She was a sensual woman, with a woman's desires. And no man but Sam had ever touched her.

He lifted the bottom of her T-shirt, and Cassie raised herself from the floor long enough for him to pull it up. She couldn't let him do this. Had to stop him.

Sometime.

She was so tired of fighting. Of being strong. Of being lonely.

His hands slid along her belly and up, until he found her unfettered breasts.

Cassie gasped as his hands took possession of her, squeezing gently, molding, stroking.

"You have no idea how many dreams I've had about these," Sam growled, lowering his head to suckle her nipple.

Sensation shot through Cassie, making her wild with need. For more. She spread her legs, lifted her hips, whimpering.

They'd first made love when they were seventeen, and after they were married it was often twice a day. The hunger had never lessened. Cassie had known, from the very first time, that it was her destiny to be sexually connected with Sam. It was as though their bodies instinctively recognized each other.

"You've grown a little," Sam muttered as his mouth moved to her other breast. "But your shape is still as perfect as ever."

He cupped both breasts, looking at them with hungry eyes. "God, I've missed this…."

Afraid of what else he might say, afraid she might have to think, Cassie lifted her hips again.

"I'm getting there, my love," Sam said, grinning. "I'm just enjoying the journey."

His grin melted her all over again. "You're overdressed."

Sam slid her T-shirt up and over her head as he stood up. The air was cool on her exposed skin, and Cassie suddenly felt naked, half sitting there on her living-room floor with her breasts in full view.

Very naked, and very, very much alive.

Watching as Sam tore his own shirt over his head, she sucked in a tight breath. He'd always been sculpted like a work of art, but because of the years of manual labor, his upper body now brought art to a whole new level.

"You've got chest hair," she said, her voice thick. He'd had only a little the last time she'd seen him naked.

He ran one hand over his chest. "It happens," he said.

"I like it." Her fingers were itching to run

through it, her breasts already tingling as she thought about that wiry roughness rubbing against her.

His hands moved to the button on his fly, and Cassie's hands began to shake. Her body grew moist in ways it hadn't been in years. She'd forgotten how incredible sexual desire could be. How all-consuming.

She'd never forgotten how great sex with Sam could be.

The rasp of his zipper increased her anticipation, and Cassie almost wept with the wanting. She'd never known such powerful need. Never even imagined she could feel so aroused.

He could ask her to do anything at that moment—run naked in the street, climb a tree topless—and if he'd appease the desire burning inside her, she'd definitely do it.

"Please, Sam," she whispered, watching his hands as he slowly drew his pants down over the bulge under his fly.

Sam had been a mere twenty years old when he'd left town. He'd come back a full-grown man.

Tears sprang to Cassie's eyes as he revealed his erection—hard and proud. Kicking off his sandals, he dropped his pants and came back to her, completely naked. Completely man. Completely perfect.

He started to say something, but Cassie couldn't

bear any more words, any more fear. She had to have this tension abated, to find the release that only Sam could give her. To know again the excitement—and the peace—his body brought hers. Lifting her head, she kissed him hotly, opening her mouth, searching his tongue with her own.

"God, Cassie, slow down..." he said.

He slid down her body, kissing her all over—her neck, her breasts, her belly, stopping where her shorts still covered her hips. Her legs, shamelessly open, tensed as she felt his hand cup her most private place.

"Ohhhh," she breathed out, then took in a couple of short, gulping breaths.

Sam moved again, frustrating Cassie. He'd been so close. Had he no idea that she was dying for him?

With one finger he flipped open her shorts, then yanked softly, pulling them slowly down her legs. For an instant she panicked, knowing almost subconsciously that this was dangerous. That she was muddying waters that were already so murky she could hardly pass through them. But on a conscious level, she just needed him to hurry. Before she lost her mind with want. Before she had to *think*.

And besides, the scar was craftily hidden in her pubic hair line. Her doctor had been quick to assure her of that. There was no need to bring any of that history here, tonight.

He sat between her legs, looking down at her, and started to gently, reverently fondle her, using both hands to bring her to the brink.

Because he was Sam, because her body recognized him, she felt no shyness, no embarrassment in having him sit there, having him see her. Instead, it felt natural. And free.

"Please, Sam," she finally begged, lifting her hips against his fingers. "Please, now."

She couldn't hold on any longer. She was going to burst into tears if he didn't relieve the agony he'd created. Her arms and legs were trembling, her lower belly quivering with need. She could hardly breathe.

With a hand on either side of her, Sam rose to his knees and then lowered himself, finding her instantly. He pushed. Hard.

And Cassie exploded.

There was pain—it would have been impossible not to experience some discomfort after ten years of celibacy—but the ecstasy was so encompassing that Cassie almost welcomed the discomfort as a way to measure the boundless pleasure.

Sam pulled out and pushed again. And again. Moving faster as his breathing quickened. His body slick with sweat, he hovered over her, and Cassie met him thrust for thrust, building to a crescendo a second time.

When they reached it together, the glory was un-

fathomable. Cassie floated almost to a state of un-
consciousness as wave after wave of pleasure
washed over her. Through her. She could feel
Sam's body flooding her, could feel his heart
pounding above her. Wondered how one ever recovered from such a moment.

Even they had never done anything so incredible
before.

And most assuredly never would again.

Because it wasn't real.

SAM WAS STILL DRIFTING on a sea of blissful sensation, when Cassie moved beneath him, pushing
him away.

"Sorry, honey," he said, instantly contrite. He
knew he must be crushing her. He rolled to one
side, only briefly aware of the rug burns on his
knees, taking her with him. He hoped her backside
had fared better.

His arms enfolded her, but Cassie didn't relax
against him. Her body was tense, nothing like the
limp, satiated woman she used to be after they
made love. She pushed against him again until he
had to let her go.

"What's wrong?" he asked, his stomach knotting.

She reached for her shirt. "Nothing." The word
was muffled as she pulled the T-shirt over her head.
In record time, she had her shorts on, too.

Frowning, Sam sat there, naked, watching her. Something was not right. "Talk to me, Cass," he said.

She shook her head. "I think you should go."

Staring at her, he continued to sit on her floor. "I don't believe this."

Her back to him, Cassie didn't answer. She was struggling, he knew that much; he just didn't know why.

"What was this?" he asked, emotions on overload as the peace of moments ago was shattered. "A quick screw for old times' sake?"

If this reversal of hers hadn't been so ironically cruel, to both of them, he never would have said such a thing. He hated hearing the words roll off his tongue. But he was falling apart, here.

He'd thought he and Cassie—the only woman to whom he'd ever given his heart and soul—had recommitted themselves to a love that had never died. She'd been...

What? What had she been doing?

Cassie stood a few feet away, her back still turned, her shoulders slumped beneath the tangled red hair. He couldn't tell if she was crying or not, but he had a feeling she was. He had a feeling he was, too.

"I'm sorry," he said softly. "I didn't mean that."

Though she didn't turn around, Cassie nodded.

"Please go." The words were whispered, and hinted of tears.

Sam stood, pulled on his pants. "I can't, Cassie. Not like this. Not until we talk."

She turned then. He'd been right about the tears.

"There's nothing to say, Sam," she said. The certainty behind those words cut him badly.

"Of course there is! We just made incredible love, Cassie."

"It changes nothing." At least she hadn't tried to deny his assertion.

"It changes everything."

Cassie shook her head, sniffling. "It doesn't, Sam. It can't."

He reached for a tissue from the table beside the couch, crossed over to gently wipe away her tears. "Of course it can, honey. We have a gift, you and I, a tangible connection that can't be broken."

She backed away from him. "It *was* broken, Sam," she said firmly. "You broke it."

Frustrated, frightened, Sam stared at her, not knowing what to do. But knowing he had to do something. He couldn't let her confine them to a life of emptiness because of one mistake he'd made when he was little more than a kid.

"Can we talk about it, Cass? Can we talk about that night?"

Her beautiful brown eyes filled with tears as she sat down on the couch, gazing up at him. "What's there to say?'' she asked. ''While I waited at home, worried sick about you, you were in bed with another woman. End of story.''

Sam swallowed. He'd hurt her beyond measure. He'd known that. But to be face to face with that fact made him feel that raw pain all over again.

''We weren't in bed.'' He regretted the stupid words the second they left his mouth. He had no idea what to say. How to atone for what he'd done. And yet, he was a good man. A faithful man. If she could only give him a second chance. Give *them* a second chance. After the way they'd just made love, the things her body and heart had told him, he knew he wasn't the only one who was going to lose one of life's greatest gifts if she couldn't move beyond the past.

''I don't care where you were.'' She enunciated carefully, bitterness in her voice, in the wet eyes that tortured him. ''You had sex with her.''

He'd give his life to be able to deny that statement. But he couldn't.

''I was drunk, Cassie, and strangling on the expectations here. I knew that if we continued as we were, I was going to disappoint you. There was just no way I could be the man you—and everyone else in this town—wanted.''

''Was she worth it, Sam?''

''Worth *what*, dammit?'' He strode over to haul her into his arms, to remind her of what they'd just shared, what they had—but when she shrank back, he stopped short of the couch. "She was nothing, Cassie, nothing. A stupid attempt to find mindlessness. To convince myself that I could act outside all those expectations."

Cassie wouldn't meet his eyes.

"I don't even remember what she looked like," he added.

But he'd remembered every inch of Cassie's body. Every touch. Every scent. He'd noticed changes, too. A little more shape. A line or two that hadn't been there before.

"Was she good?" The question was so softly uttered, Sam barely heard it.

"How would I know Cassie? I was too drunk to care. I don't even remember her. How 'good' could it have been?"

But he'd remembered the feel of Cassie's long legs against the sides of his hips, her tender flesh wrapped intimately around him. He'd remembered the look in her eyes when she came, the sensual smile on her lips. He'd remembered how she'd said his name with that breathless throaty growl.

Sam kneeled in front of her, wanting so desperately to touch her, to take both her hands in his. "Please, Cass," he whispered, "can you please try to forgive me? I'll do anything, promise you anything, call you every time I leave the house, carry a pager and a cell phone and be accountable to you every single second, if that's what it takes to win back your trust.''

She still wouldn't look at him, but she seemed to be listening. ''That night wasn't about sex Cass,'' he said. ''I don't really know what it *was* about...'' He paused. ''Maybe it was about freedom,'' he said quietly.

Her eyes instantly clouded again. ''You needed to be free from me?''

''Not from you,'' Sam said. ''Never from you. But from *here,* maybe. And from the things you needed me to be.''

She digested the words silently.

''It was about my life, Cass. About finding answers. It was never about sex.'' He inhaled a deep breath, knowing this might be his one and only chance to reach her. ''I've found my answers, know who I am and where I'm going. And I know that you're the only woman who's ever turned me on to the point of forgetfulness.'' He was giving her everything, laying it all at her feet. She deserved that from him. ''I swear to you I will never, ever need another woman the way I need you. I will never again make love to another woman as long as I'm with you.''

Cassie turned away from him, but not before he'd seen the fresh tears come to her eyes.

''But you've been with other women, haven't you?'' she asked. ''In your years away.''

"Not for a long time, honey. Not since I knew there was no point. You were always the woman in my heart."

Her shoulders held stiffly, she didn't respond.

"Can you honestly tell me the love is gone, Cass?" he asked, risking everything. Was he just kidding himself about the connection between them? The spiritual and physical communion they'd just shared?

"It's too late, Sam," she said.

"I can't believe that."

She hadn't denied her love for him. Intuitively, Sam understood that she couldn't.

During his years away, he hadn't always been sure of the bond they shared, but now that he was back, now that he'd seen her again, he knew for certain that what he and Cassie had was stronger than life. Stronger than death.

"Please, just go."

Sam kneeled there a while longer, watching her. In all that time, she didn't speak another word, but her rigid shoulders told him that what she'd said was true: she needed him to go. His presence here was only causing her more heartache.

He'd promised himself he wouldn't do that.

"Okay, I'm going," he said, standing, pulling on his shirt, slipping his feet into his sandals. "But I'm not deserting you again, Cass. I love you. And

someday, somehow, I'm going to prove that to
you.''

CASSIE WAITED until she heard Sam's truck drive
away before she dared to move. Almost immediately, panic set in, taking her breath, her ability to
think. She had to get help.

Phyllis would have been a likely candidate, but
right now Cassie needed someone who'd already
seen her at her worst. Someone she'd trusted for
years with her deepest secrets. Someone who
wouldn't make her talk about things she couldn't
face.

Barefoot and braless, she scrambled frantically
around her house, until she remembered that she'd
left her purse in the bedroom. She grabbed it, fum-
bled inside, spilling stuff on the floor until she
pulled out her keys.

Thank God, Randi and Zack lived so close. She
could make it the couple of blocks from her house
to theirs. It was the middle of the night. Shelter
Valley streets would be deserted.

She had to get to Zack.

SOMETIME AFTER TWO in the morning, a very disheveled but partially dressed Zack Foster answered
his door, still too sleepy to wonder who was there.
Sammie was barking beside him. Bear, sleeping in
the corner of the foyer, opened one lazy eye. Brat

was barking from her kennel in the laundry room, which was right where the dalmatian puppy was going to stay.

He was instantly wide awake when he saw his partner standing barefoot on his porch, her hair a mess.

"Cass?" He flipped on the porch light as he swung the door open. "What's happened?" he asked, his arm around her before the door had even shut.

"Cassie?" Randi met them in the hallway, pulling on a pair of gym shorts. "What's wrong?"

When Cassie burst into tears, Zack's alarm grew.

"I slept with him."

His eyes met Randi's over Cassie's bent head. Hers said *I told you so.* Zack's heart sank.

"You're a grown woman, Cass," Randi said, running one hand lightly along Cassie's arm. "You're allowed to do those things."

Zack's look told Randi in no uncertain terms to shut up.

"Not with Sam," she said, trying to regain control but not succeeding. Her hair was hanging in her face. Her makeup had long since worn away. Her face was tear-streaked, her expression anguished.

The way she looked brought back memories of old times. Old and very difficult times. Zack was going to kill Sam Montford.

He guided Cassie to the couch in the living room, and he and Randi sat on either side of her. Randi handed her a tissue. Sammie settled at Cassie's feet.

"How'd it happen?" he asked her softly.

"Do you really need to ask?" Randi frowned. "Surely you've figured that out by now."

Zack knew that Randi didn't think Sam and Cassie together was bad news. She'd been predicting this exact outcome for more than a week. Had a bet with Zack, as a matter of fact, a bet he'd just lost. But he didn't care about any bet with his wife at the moment. What he did care about was his partner's emotional health. She'd fought a long, hard fight to achieve calm and contentment—and then her ex-husband showed up.

"He came over to tell me about Mariah's attack," Cassie finally said.

Zack nodded. Sam had been distraught, and Zack should've have guessed where the man would go for solace. Zack had sought Cassie's strength himself, back when he'd been struggling with the break-up of his first marriage—struggling with his own sense of identity upon discovering that his first wife was leaving him for another woman.

Cassie had kept him sane back then. It was up to him to keep her sane now.

"How is Mariah?" he asked. One thing at a time. She was calmer. That was the first step.

"Okay." Cassie nodded her head once, still

looking down at her lap. "There's nothing physically wrong with her. She's sedated for the night and has an appointment in Phoenix on Monday."

"Poor thing," Randi said. "Her little heart was beating faster than a bird's."

Zack still felt sick every time he thought about the debilitating fear he'd seen in Sam's daughter that afternoon. He'd felt so helpless, so powerless to do anything. By the look of things, Sam Montford had been feeling the same, but on a bigger scale.

"So how did you get from Mariah's attack to sleeping with him?" Zack asked. No matter how much Sam might be suffering, Zack couldn't feel any real softening toward the guy. His job was to protect Cassie.

Cassie shrugged. "I don't know." She started to cry softly again. Jumping off the couch, she paced around the living room. Sammie sat at attention, watching her. "I guess because I'm a weak fool."

Randi shook her head. "Or in love."

"How can she love him?" Zack asked his wife. "He ran out on her, left her alone to deal with—"

"And now he's back," Randi interrupted. "I have no idea why Sam did what he did," she said to Zack, but she was watching Cassie, too. "I do know that up until the point where he screwed up, he was the most reliable kid any of us knew. And it was also obvious that he adored Cassie. You don't just walk away from that if you have a chance to make it right.''

"I think you'd just like to see everyone as happy as we are," Zack said quietly.

"He said the town put too many expectations on him," Cassie told them suddenly, frowning as she looked at Randi. Cassie was tearing a tissue apart, stuffing the pieces into her palm. "He didn't want to go into law or politics. The thought of working at Montford, Inc. all day, every day for the rest of his life was killing him. He tried to talk about it— I remember him saying things to me, to his parents, but they just thought he was blowing off steam. I guess I took my cues from them. We all thought he *wanted* the life that had been planned for him. He fit into that mold so perfectly.''

Randi nodded. "It must've been tough growing up the way he did, with everyone deciding who he was going to be the day he was born. The poor guy never had a chance.''

Didn't sound like a whole lot of fun to Zack. What man wouldn't have to fight back?

"He should've gone to Cassie. Not to the arms of another woman," Zack insisted.

"But weren't you encouraging him to go to law school, just like everyone else?" Randi asked Cassie. "Maybe even expecting it?''

Cassie shrugged, her expression confused.

"Maybe. Because that seemed to be the plan. But it never dawned on me that he wouldn't want to."

"He was young, too, Cassie," Randi said softly. "Maybe he didn't feel you were really hearing him. Maybe he didn't trust you enough to love him for what he *was,* not for what everyone thought he was going to be. Or maybe he just didn't want to subject you to an entirely different life than the one you wanted—the one you signed on for."

They were silent for a couple of minutes. Zack was looking for a solution, but the whole thing appeared to be one big screw-up. A lose-lose situation, if he ever saw one. Sam had loved Cassie back then. Cassie had loved Sam. In one way they'd been so close; but in another, their lives were careering in different directions.

And so much had happened since then. So many irrevocable hurts.

"Now what?" he asked.

Cassie tried to smile. "Life goes on."

Randi threw up her hands. "That's it? You sleep with him...and nothing?"

"What else is there?"

"I don't know. Love, maybe."

"Don't you see," Cassie asked, her eyes beseeching as she gazed from one to the other.

For the first time, Zack understood what Randi had seen all along. Cassie still loved her ex-husband. Desperately.

"It doesn't matter if I love him or not. I can't trust him. And I can't forgive him, either."

"For sleeping with another woman?" Randi asked.

Cassie shook her head, and Zack knew what was coming.

"For deserting me when I needed him most." The words choked her. "I was a little over two months pregnant when Sam left town."

Randi sat stock-still. "I'd heard something about a baby," she whispered.

"Largely due to the stress of Sam's betrayal and desertion, I had a lot of problems with the pregnancy." She stopped. Took a deep breath. "My daughter died," Cassie said, her voice breaking.

Zack waited for the rest. The worst part of all.

"And after it was all over, they told me I can't have any more children."

"Does Sam know?" Randi asked.

Shaking her head, Cassie sniffled, reached for a fresh tissue.

"So you tell him," Randi said, exasperating Zack with her optimism. And captivating him, as well. "And then you adopt!"

Even as Zack tried to catch Randi's eye, to tell her to shut up, Cassie said, "I can't be with Sam."

"Why not?" Randi's brows drew together.

"Because although I know logically that Sam's not to blame for Emily's death, my heart still says he is. And I can't forgive him for that."

CHAPTER FOURTEEN

SAM WAS UP ALL NIGHT. The newcomer to Borough Bantam had a plan now. But as was the case with all worthy undertakings, the way was not yet clear. The creatures in the kingdom scurried around as they'd done for years, each week bringing some new crisis that seemed so huge to them and so small to the reader.

To them, all of life was right there in the Borough, their little problems and triumphs of utmost importance. The stories were satirical, and yet the residents of Borough Bantam somehow managed to teach Sam every single week. Essential truths. Life lessons that Sam had learned in Shelter Valley. Lessons he'd taken with him without even realizing it.

He figured his readers must see the value in them, too, since the comic strip was unbelievably successful.

I am. I am. I am. And then in the bottom corner, *S.N.C.* Sam dropped his pencil. There was something so reassuring about that damn worm.

If he could only figure why, Sam knew he'd have a major problem solved. But as always, the answer eluded him. He folded up the drawings, put them in their envelope and cleaned up, slipping his satchel on the back of the closet shelf.

Borough Bantam was just one more thing the people of Shelter Valley would never understand.

They'd think he was poking fun at them. When in reality he was giving the rest of the world what everyone here in this small town had already discovered. The secrets to a happy life.

TWO WEEKS PASSED, and Cassie managed to keep up such an effective semblance of normalcy, she almost convinced herself that she'd survived her weak moment with Sam unscathed.

If only she didn't have to go to bed at night. To sleep. That was where the memories, the desires, and especially the unending regrets attacked her. If she slept, she dreamed. If she was awake, she thought of nothing else. Round and round. How could something be so right and so completely impossible at the same time? How could the same man make her feel so wonderful, so right inside—and so endlessly distraught?

And more to the point, what did she do about it? He'd been patient with her, bringing Mariah for her sessions four times now without any pressure. Not asking anything of her other than that she help his little girl. There'd been no more surprise visits to her house. And when she'd run into him at the diner last week, he'd been congenial. And had left her alone.

She missed him like crazy.

And yet she was relieved.

She was going to have to tell him about their baby. About Emily. There was just no other way to get beyond this whole mess. To find a peaceful place to exist for the rest of her life. She had to get it all out. And she needed him to know.

But not yet. Not until she could at least think about going through that without falling apart. Without accusing him of killing their daughter and destroying any chance she'd ever have of having another child.

Logically, she knew he wasn't really responsible. Any more than she'd been. But in her heart, she also knew that if Sam hadn't deserted her, Emily's chances would have been so much better....

Now, a tiny, almost imperceptible tug on her hand brought Cassie back to the present. Dressed in navy shorts and a white button-up blouse with the sleeves rolled up, her hair in its usual twist, she was walking down Main Street with Mariah. They were on their way to Weber's Department Store, where she was going to buy the little girl a new dress.

She glanced down at her charge. "Did you want something, Mariah?" The little girl slowed as Cassie slowed, stopped as Cassie stopped, but there was no response.

Thinking the child must have tripped, Cassie started to walk again. "You hot, Sammie girl?" Cassie asked.

Panting, the dog looked up at her, but continued trotting beside Mariah. If Sammie was uncomfortable, she didn't seem aware of it.

"What color dress do you want, sweetie?" Cassie asked the little girl. She might as well have been talking to herself. There was no way to be sure the child listened, or comprehended much of what was said to her.

Cassie wondered if the shopping spree was such a great idea. Mariah didn't need any new clothes. She always looked very cute. Today her long black hair hung in two braids down her back, and the little brightly flowered sundress matched her sandals perfectly. They probably wouldn't find anything that fashionable at Weber's. But Cassie was hoping Mariah might enjoy their expedition. Or, at least, find a different environment interesting.

There hadn't been any reaction from Mariah since her "episode," but the child didn't seem to have gone backward, either. There'd been no resistance to their outings. No more shaking.

The one thing Mariah did seem to respond to was Sammie. If you watched closely enough to tell.

"Wouldn't you hate to be wearing all that fur

Sammie's got on?'' Cassie asked Mariah. The child walked steadily, but she wasn't staring as vacantly as usual. She seemed almost to be sneaking peeks sideways.

Cassie walked a little faster. And felt another little squeeze on her hand.

Heart beating rapidly, she stopped again, certain now that Mariah was trying to tell her something. ''What is it, honey?'' she asked, kneeling in front the child.

Mariah's stare instantly became vacant again. But her hand was rubbing Sammie's fur agitatedly. The dog looked over at Cassie, as though expecting some kind of action from her.

Cassie wished the dog could talk. Could tell her what to do. There was no visible sign of distress on the little girl's face, and Cassie straightened. ''You just tell me if you need something, Mariah,'' she said. ''Now, how about we go find some new clothes?'' With the child's hand still in hers, Cassie started to walk.

The child refused to move.

Cassie knelt down again. ''Sweetie, you can trust me,'' she said. ''We've been together a lot. I bring Sammie to you every time, and you like Sammie, don't you?''

Mariah didn't even blink.

''Whatever's bothering you, try to let me know. I'll help you.''

Still no response. A couple of people walked by, smiled at Cassie, glanced curiously at the child, and moved on. Mariah didn't even appear to notice them.

"Do you have to go to the potty?" Cassie asked. That had never happened on Cassie's outings with the little girl. Sam always made sure she'd gone just before he brought her.

"Come on," Cassie said. "We can pop into the ice-cream shop and use the bathroom there." Mariah liked chocolate ice cream—as long as she could wait until Sam was back before she ate it. "And then we'll have to stop for a scoop of ice cream on our way out."

Mariah still refused to budge.

Elated, Cassie tried not to smile. Mariah was responding! Cassie could hardly contain her excitement.

Now, if she could just figure out what the hell Mariah was being so adamant about.

"Everything okay?" Liz Meiers, the church choir director, stopped to ask.

"Fine." *Please go away,* she begged silently. She didn't want anyone scaring the child back into her shell.

Liz moved on, and Cassie put her face close to Mariah's, trying to get the child to focus on her.

"Is it that you don't want to buy new clothes?" she asked next. "We could skip that and settle for a soda at the diner. Or stop at the dime store for some candy. We could even look at the toys.''

They could go back to the park, too, but the idea was to keep Mariah out and among the bustle of strangers. As much of a bustle as they could find in Shelter Valley, anyway.

Cassie had already tried taking the child to the clinic, but Mariah had shown no interest in being there. She'd curled up in the fetal position in a chair, one hand on Sammie, and had laid her head on her knees, waiting for Cassie to say they could go.

"You want to look at the toys?" Cassie asked a second time, starting toward the dime store.

Again, Mariah held her ground.

Cassie was thrilled Mariah was trying to communicate with her. And she felt a terrible sense of urgency, a need to figure out exactly what the child was trying to say.

"Sammie, *you* know what she wants, don't you?" Cassie said.

Mariah's hand stilled on Sammie's head, and her eyes turned to the side again.

"Sammie and I are both here, willing to help, honey. I just don't know what the problem is. Can't you please tell me?"

The child didn't respond. Didn't even blink.

They were attracting a bit of a crowd. Cassie had to get rid of these people. She had to find out what

Mariah was telling her before the child escaped inside herself again.

With Mariah's hand still firmly in hers, she turned away from the little girl, addressing the small concerned gathering quietly. "She's going to be fine, Mrs. Morten," she said to the seventyish woman, a client of Cassie's who had three cats at home. "All of you, she's going to be fine. We just need to be alone for a couple of min—"

The sound behind her was so foreign that Cassie stopped mid-sentence, frozen. Afraid to turn around.

"Sam." It came again. Very clear. And tinged with anxiety. "My daddy Sam."

Spinning, Cassie stared. Mariah was leaning over, her small lips barely moving as she addressed the dog at her side. She wanted Sam—her father—and she was trying to get word to Sammie without alerting anyone around her.

Tears flooded Cassie's eyes. She grabbed the child in her arms, holding her, hugging her. Whirling in a circle, while the crowd around them grew. Everyone was smiling. A few had tears in their eyes, though they probably weren't all aware of what they'd just witnessed.

"Welcome home, little Mariah," Cassie said, tears dripping unashamedly down her face. "Welcome home."

The little girl's stare was vacant again. She held

herself stiffly against Cassie. But Cassie knew they'd broken through. Mariah was coming back to them.

"You want Sam?" Cassie asked, setting the little girl down. "Then let's go find him."

Smiling at the congratulatory people around them, Cassie took Mariah's hand and started off toward the park.

The little girl jerked on Cassie's hand, pulling her around the other way.

Sharing a puzzled glance with Mrs. Morten, who waved Cassie on, Cassie allowed the child to lead her back the way they'd come, to an alley that ran between the hardware store and the dentist's office.

And there, just around the corner, where the child had probably seen him from her peripheral vision as they walked by, sat Sam on a stoop, his head in his hands. Looking like he didn't have a friend in the world.

Hearing them approach, he raised his head. The instant terror in his face as his eyes darted from Mariah to Cassie's tear-stained face tore at Cassie's heart, but all she could do was smile at him.

This was his daughter's show.

Mariah walked up to Sam, slid her tiny hand into his. And that was all. She'd obviously done what she needed to do.

Sammie sat beside Cassie, tongue hanging out of her mouth, obviously proud of her days' work.

Which left Cassie to explain.

"She said your name, Sam!" Cassie said. "She saw you sitting here! She just led me back to you! She must have thought you were in trouble, needed help. She never came after you for herself, when you left her in the park and she wanted you, but she insisted that we come for you when she thought you were in trouble!" Cassie's words tumbled out, one on top of the other.

Sam's eyes widened as he glanced quickly from her to his daughter and back again. "You're certain?"

"I heard her, Sam. She said your name twice."

Looking dazed, as though he didn't dare believe that the nightmare could be coming to an end, Sam knelt beside the child, taking both of her shoulders in his hands. "Mariah Glory Montford, if you've got words in your head, I expect to hear them," he said sternly, though his voice wobbled just a bit with emotions barely held in check.

Cassie didn't even try to wipe away the tears still dripping slowly down her cheeks. "Don't expect too much too soon," she warned him.

"When I wasn't sure she *could* talk to me, there was nothing I could do," Sam said, still watching Mariah intently, his eyes bright. "If my little girl's in there, listening to me, then I want her out here where I can have some of the fun, too."

Mariah didn't move, her face expressionless, her eyes trained on Sam's chest.

Sammie stood up, not quite at attention, but watching Mariah and Sam closely. Again, Cassie wondered how much the dog sensed.

Just when Cassie thought Mariah had given them all she had, all she could give them that day, the child's head lifted. Her eyes focused on Sam's. She didn't say anything, but there was no doubt that she was connecting.

Sam's lips trembled. And his eyes filled with tears. "Welcome back, squirt," he said, breaking into a huge smile. "I've missed you."

Gathering Mariah into his arms, he hugged her fiercely, lifting her so her legs dangled in front of him. "I've missed you *so* much." His eyes were shut tight as he buried his face against her hair.

Mariah's bony little arms stole up Sam's chest and locked themselves around his neck.

Cassie stood there watching them, and started to sob.

AT HOME THAT NIGHT, sitting in the living room with his parents, Sam was still grinning inside. Mariah was upstairs, in bed asleep. Sam had placed the receiver to the monitor system he'd bought months ago on the end table next to him. The base was upstairs right beside his sleeping daughter. He used to listen for Mariah's breathing, or any sounds of distress. Tonight, he was wondering if she just might talk in her sleep.

The three of them had yet to hear her say a word.

But you wouldn't know that, judging by the celebration held that evening. Carol, with occasional bouts of happy tears, had prepared Mariah's favorite foods—or what Sam could remember of them. Hot dogs. Mashed potatoes. Canned peaches. And for dessert, she'd made the chocolate chip cookies Sam had been telling Mariah about for months.

The child had still focused mainly on Sam's shirt. She'd sat where he put her, making no moves on her own. Except to eat. Sam hadn't had to coax her at all. With her eyes trained on him as usual, she'd dug into the food in front of her and finished every bite. It was a small thing, but to the three adults sitting at the table, who'd been holding their collective breath over every bite of every meal, it seemed a miracle.

"What did the doctor have to say?" Carol asked, her feet tucked under her violet silk lounging gown. Muffy was curled up next to her on the sofa.

Slouching in the overstuffed velvet chair across from his mother, Sam thought back to the conversation he'd had just before dinner. He'd been dying to share it with Cassie. And his parents.

"She said this is the breakthrough we've been waiting for," he told them. "She used lots of medical jargon, but the gist of it was that once Mariah starts to emerge from this catatonic state, it should be only a matter of time until she's back to normal.''

Sipping from the cup of cocoa she'd made, his mother nodded. Carol Montford, a millionaire many times over, could afford an army of household help, but—other than cleaning and laundry—insisted on doing everything herself. The shopping. The cooking. The dishes. The decorating. And making cocoa. She was addicted to her nightly cup of homemade cocoa.

"She expects full recovery, then?" James asked Sam. He wore his reading glasses, feet up on the footrest of his tipped-back easy chair, but he hadn't opened the book on his lap. He sucked on the pipe he hadn't lit in years.

Sam slid his hand down the leg of his khaki shorts. "According to her, it's very hopeful. But until we know the extent of what Mariah saw—and heard—and the extent of what she might have suffered herself at the hands of those bastards..."

"We've got her now, Sam," Carol reminded him. "And she's young. In time, those memories will fade."

Taking a deep breath, trying to rid himself of the sudden tension, Sam sent his mother a grateful smile. "I know."

Once again he realized that the people of Shelter Valley knew what really mattered in life. While

Sam sat there, consumed by the need to murder the men who had tortured and killed his best friends, while he focused on the past and the things he could do nothing to change, his mother homed right in on what was most important—the future. His daughter had been given back her life.

That was what mattered.

"Oh." Carol set down her cup. "I almost forgot in all the excitement, but this has truly been a day of happy news."

"What else happened?" Sam and his father asked together, both relaxing in their chairs, letting the day's events wash over them.

"Ben called this afternoon. He and Tory were just back from the doctor. Tory's pregnant!"

"I'll be damned," James said, sitting up a little straighter.

Sam grinned, happy for his new cousin. Now that he'd spent a little time with Ben, his cousin was growing on him. Ben had a rough time growing up, from the sound of it, sacrificed a lot. Sam wished him and Tory the best.

"Another Montford," James said, his pipe in his raised hand as he pondered the good news. "How do you like that, Carol?" He smiled at his wife. "A year ago, we were two lonely old coots thinking we might've seen everything life had to offer—and look at us now. Two sons—" he glanced at Sam "—or damn close to it, two grandkids and another on the way. Goes to show that you can't give up.

As long as you're kicking, there could be a surprise waiting around the corner. A surprise of the pleasant variety.''

The intimate look his parents shared could have seemed exclusive, but somehow it didn't make Sam feel shut out. He just felt damn lucky to be sitting there, part of this family. Loved.

"You're right, of course," Carol said. "As always. Gets a bit hard to take now and then, you know?" she teased, her expression changing to an impish grin. "You always being right, I mean."

Nearly seventy years old, and looking impish. Sam filed that away. Borough Bantam needed that grin.

"Now, if only I could convince the rest of the world…" James said, pretending to frown as he slipped his pipe back between his teeth.

"You ready for more news?" Carol asked.

"There's more?" Sam asked. James raised his eyebrows.

"There is." Carol nodded, grinning as she drew out the suspense. "Ben was telling me that Zack and Randi just found out that they're expecting, too.''

"No kidding," James said contentedly. "Life is good, isn't it, Carol.''

Sam probably would have filed away that reaction, too. But he was trying too hard to keep himself from darting out of his chair and into the night. His mother's last piece of news had made him wonder what was in the air. If babies were contagious.

That fanciful thought led to another—this one much more alarming. He knew how babies were made. And he and Cassie had done a fine job of illustrating that process a couple of weeks before. Without protection of any kind.

He'd been so caught up in all the emotional intensity surrounding that night. And he'd been used to making love to her without thoughts of birth control—after all, ten years ago they'd been hoping for a large family, the sooner the better—that the possibility of a baby hadn't dawned on him until this very moment.

Cassie was as regular as clockwork. Surely she'd have said something if it was the fertile part of her cycle. But there were always other factors to consider. Emotional upsets that changed timing.

He had to get over to her. Talk about that night. About possible repercussions. He had to take full responsibility. Giving her time was no longer an option.

"Think I'll go for a drive, if you two don't mind." He tried to keep the words casual. He certainly didn't need his parents suspecting anything— not until he'd spoken to Cassie.

He wondered if they could see his heart pounding in his chest.

"Don't hurt her, son."

James's warning followed him out into the night.

CHAPTER FIFTEEN

"YOU WANT TO COME IN and see a movie?" Phyllis asked as Cassie dropped her off after dinner in Phoenix on Friday night.

Cassie shook her head. "Thanks, but I'm in the middle of a dried-flower découpage on my kitchen wall. I want to get the first coat done tonight so it has time to dry before tomorrow."

Opening the passenger door of Cassie's Taurus, Phyllis said, "Well, dinner was a great idea. Thanks for asking me."

"Thanks for coming," Cassie replied. "I really needed to talk."

Climbing out, Phyllis turned and leaned against the door frame. "Yeah, well, you're also a good listener, Cassie. Do you want to do this again?"

"Are you kidding?" Cassie asked. "I was wondering if next week would be too soon for a repeat performance. There's that new Greek place we passed on the north side of Phoenix."

"How's Friday night?"

"Great!"

"I'll call you later in the week to set a time,"

Phyllis said. Then she added, "You take care, okay?"

Cassie put the car in gear. "I will."

"Call if you need me...."

Feeling more in control than she had in a long time, Cassie drove home, a Supertramp CD blaring on her stereo. *"Know who you are,"* she sang along.

It was advice she was working on. But not something she was certain she'd ever fully achieve. There were so many facets to life, so many roles to play, so many changes to adjust to—could anyone ever know who he or she really was?

And what about Phyllis? She seemed content with her life, had a meaningful career, was a good friend to so many people in this town. Yet when she'd talked tonight there'd been an underlying emptiness. She might assert that she was happy without a man in her life. But Cassie believed Phyllis wanted to be in a relationship and was scared to death to try again.

And who could blame her? She'd had her heart broken, not because of something she'd done but because of who she *was*.

As she considered this, Cassie suddenly frowned. Somebody was sitting on her front steps; she saw him when she passed her house on the way to her driveway. She didn't need to spot Sam's truck out by her garage to know it was him.

She wasn't really surprised. After the breakthrough they'd had with Mariah that afternoon, she'd been half expecting him to show up. Sam never seemed to just pick up a phone.

Now that she thought about it, he'd rarely called her when they were young. He'd always just appeared on her doorstep. Or at her locker, or her softball game, or her pew at church, or the grocery store where she'd worked for a while as a kid...

And she'd always been thrilled to see him.

But as she'd said before, *that was then*. This was now.

"How is she?" she asked in lieu of hello. She walked around to her front porch, joining him on the steps.

He was still wearing the shorts and white polo shirt he'd had on that afternoon. Cassie, having changed for her trip to Phoenix, felt overdressed by comparison in her form-fitting, short navy dress.

"She's asleep," Sam said. "But she ate every bite of her dinner."

"Did you talk to her doctor?"

Sam nodded, then gave Cassie a full report. Although he remained noticeably happy about the day's events, he seemed to have something else on his mind. He wasn't really meeting her eyes, was spending more time looking at the palm leaf between his fingers than at her.

He was making Cassie nervous.

"Did Mariah say any more?"

Sam shook his head. "Not yet, but it'll come."

Gazing out over her yard, Cassie said softly, "Be prepared. When she does start talking, I suspect she'll have some pretty horrible stories to tell."

"She may not remember them." But his protest was half-hearted.

"She remembers, Sam. You just have to look at that solemn little face to know."

He didn't argue.

The night air was hot—hotter than usual for May. Cassie felt a drop of sweat trickle between her breasts. Why was Sam just sitting here?

She wasn't going to invite him in. She couldn't.

"We need to talk, Cassie," he finally said, his voice firm.

"Okay." She wasn't sure what he thought they had to talk about. They'd already been over things. Gotten nowhere.

"Zack and Randi are expecting a baby."

"I know." The two of them had been like kids when they'd come in to tell Cassie the day before. She'd been the first to know.

And she'd been so happy for them, she'd worn a smile for the rest of the day. Right up until she'd come home last night...and remembered that she would never again know the joy of having a life growing inside her. Would never again experience that sweet anticipation Zack and Randi were now sharing. Never know the wonder of—

"Ben and Tory are expecting, too."

"No kidding!" She hadn't heard that. But she was happy for them, too. If anyone deserved a miracle, it was Tory Sanders. Cassie really admired the woman. Coming from an abusive past involving both her stepfather and her first husband, she'd managed to retain a sense of self—and an ability to love.

"We have to talk, Cassie."

He'd already said that.

She waited. And suddenly wished she hadn't eaten that order of honey chicken for dinner.

"When's your next period?"

Cassie choked on the breath she'd been sucking in. "Excuse me?"

"Have you had one since I was here last?"

"Nooo." Like it was any of his business anymore.

Then it dawned on her where he was going.

"I didn't even think to use protection that night, Cass. Did you?" He turned his head, trying to meet her eyes in the glow from the streetlight.

Cassie looked away. "I didn't think at all that night."

"So we could be expecting, too."

"We aren't." Staring into the night, she had a

sudden urge to run. To lose herself in the darkness. "If that's why you're worried, don't be."

Dropping the palm leaf, Sam threaded his fingers, elbows on his knees. "You just said you haven't had a period yet."

"I haven't, but..." Cassie searched for something to convince him. "The timing's not right." Something aside from the truth. She wasn't ready for that.

"So you'll be starting some time this next week?"

Okay, sure. "I guess." Since Emily, she hadn't been regular.

"And what if you don't?"

Cassie pulled her knees up to her chest, hugging them. She could think of only one conversation that could be worse. The one where he found out what he'd really left behind ten years ago.

"Then I'll have it the week after that," she snapped. Discussing her personal functions with him was far too intimate.

But more frightening was the direction in which they were heading. She had to tell him sometime. Not because he had a right to know; he'd lost that right when he'd abandoned her.

She needed him to know for *her*. So *she* could leave it all behind and move on for good. Her talks with Phyllis—and with Zack—had helped her see that. But she needed more time—

"And what if you don't?" Sam's voice broke into her thoughts.

"Don't what?"

"Have your period the week after that."

"Don't worry, I'll have it."

His hands still clasped in front of him, staring out at the street, Sam said, "I think we should get married."

"What?" Her voice was much louder than she'd intended.

"You might be pregnant, Cassie. I think we should get married."

He'd lost his mind.

Or she had.

"We've already done that. It's not something I care to repeat."

And yet...she did. Marriage to Sam was all she'd ever wanted. The Sam she'd seen these past weeks, loving his daughter, his parents. Doing little things to make her life easier. Appreciating the people of Shelter Valley. Playing basketball with his cousin, and her best friends.

It was the other parts of him that she couldn't bring herself to love again. He'd been unfaithful to her. Left her alone to deal with the birth—and death—of their child. How did a woman ever forget that? Or forgive it?

"We still love each other, Cassie," he said now.

She could hear the frustration creeping into his voice.

She opened her mouth to deny what he'd said. Except that she couldn't. The night they'd made love again had made it impossible to deny that Sam still had power over her heart.

And he knew that, dammit.

"I'm not marrying you again."

"I'm not giving up on us."

Stalemate.

"Go home, Sam," Cassie said wearily. "You've got Mariah to concentrate on right now. She needs you."

"She needs you, too."

Cassie wasn't so sure about that. "It was Sammie she spoke to," she reminded him. "Which is something I've been meaning to talk to you about. Now that she's beginning to recover, you really should get her a dog of her own. One she knows is hers, part of her family, sharing her daily life. The sooner the better. Before she gets too attached to Sammie."

"Mightn't it already be too late?" Sam asked. She could see his brow crease in the dim light.

Cassie shook her head. "I don't think so. She's hardly even looked at Sammie. Right now, Sammie's just a dog. I don't think the particulars mattered. But they probably will from now on."

He turned his head toward her again. "You know anyone who might have a puppy for us, Doc?"

"I just might." Cassie folded her hands, clenching them to stop their trembling. "The litter my puppy's coming from is just being weaned. The puppies should be ready to leave their mother by next week. Last I heard, there was still one available. I can get you the owner's number on Monday, if you'd like."

"Thanks." And then he added, "You think Muffy'll be okay with another dog around?"

"Her nose might be out of joint for the first while, but as long as she still gets lots of attention, she'll probably just take the little one under her wing."

Silence fell, each of them staring out at the empty street. The family in the house across from hers went to bed. Cassie watched their upstairs lights go out, one by one.

Would Sam leave now?

"If you're pregnant, we should get married right away." Sam's low voice was startling in the silence.

Cassie swallowed. If he kept this up forever, could she keep fighting him forever? Did she have any other choice?

"I'm not going to marry you again."

"If you're pregnant—"

"I'm not pregnant," she interrupted sharply.

He turned to face her, his hand brushing her cheek briefly before dropping against his knee. "You don't know that for sure, Cass. If—"

"I do know for sure, Sam." She bit the words out. Whether she was ready or not, she couldn't keep this in anymore. "In fact, I couldn't be more sure."

He frowned, his head tilted as he tried to read the expression she was trying just as hard to hide. "What do you mean by that?"

"I can't have children, Sam," she said through gritted teeth. "Ever." All the agony she'd been struggling to subdue rose up to choke her. Telling Sam made it...final.

Because Sam was the only man she wanted to have a baby with.

Bitter tears spilled down her cheeks, and as Sam reached over to wipe them away with the pad of his thumb, Cassie bowed her head. She couldn't share even her tears with him. Couldn't have him trying to make it better.

He was ten years too late.

SAM FROZE, his hand suspended above Cassie's bent head, staring at her. She wasn't making any sense.

"Run that by me again?" He hadn't meant to whisper, but that was how the words came out.

"I can't have children."

Oh, God. Cassie infertile? That news must have killed her. Cassie had always wanted babies of her own. Sam ached for her.

"Why not?" His throat was dry.

"Scarring."

She was still crying. He could hear the tears in her voice. And felt so helpless. How could he fix this one?

"Scarring where? From what?" Maybe there was a specialist somewhere. They had the money; there had to be some way to help her.

But if this horrible thing was true, he now understood the emptiness he'd sensed in Cassie's life. In her heart. It wasn't just a matter of regaining her trust. This was much bigger. Much worse. She might still love him, but would that be enough? Marriage without the children she'd always wanted. Was this why she couldn't contemplate marrying again? Couldn't marry him—or anyone.

Were they destined to a life apart, after all, no matter how deeply they loved each other? Sam didn't want to believe that.

He'd asked about the scarring. She hadn't answered his question.

"Scarring from what, Cassie? How long ago? With all of today's new technologies—laser surgery and so on—maybe there's something that can be done."

Cassie's head shot up, her gaze locking with his,

and Sam felt the shock of that look deep inside him. They weren't in this together. He was the enemy.

"It was ten years ago," she said, her voice hard, accusing. "And the scarring...was caused by...the problems I had when I—" She stopped, took a breath shuddering with sobs. "When I gave birth to our daughter."

Sam's heart stopped beating. He stared at her, numb. Her blunt words slammed into him over and over again.

This wasn't happening. This whole nightmare just wasn't happening.

He was vaguely aware of Cassie crying beside him, could feel her body next to him, shaking with sobs. Instinctively, he reached out to put his arm around her. To pull her close while they figured out what to do.

She shrugged him off.

"We had a daughter," he said woodenly. It didn't make sense. Wasn't real.

Cassie nodded. Her head bowed as she cried softly.

"Where is she?"

Cassie looked up then, and the agony in her eyes reverberated inside him. Somehow, he was responsible for this.

"Shall I take you to her, Sam?" she asked, tears pouring freely down her face.

Not in all his years of dealing with tragedies had he felt such utter despair.

"Please," he said slowly. Wherever his daughter was, he wanted to be with her. Wanted to share her with Cassie.

Shoulders slumped, Cassie walked slowly back to her car, climbed in and turned on the ignition, waiting only until Sam had shut the passenger door before shooting off down the drive.

Where was she, this child of his? Was she in a hospital, an institution? Where was she that, without any warning, they could go and see her after ten o'clock at night?

A horrible, logical possibility lodged itself in the back of his mind, but Sam couldn't acknowledge it.

"What's her name?" he asked, staring out the windshield, not blinking.

"Emily."

He could tell that talking was difficult for her, so he just let her drive, his mind scrambling furiously to work out what might lie ahead. And how he could somehow help them both through this. How he might make up to Cassie for whatever hell he had left her to deal with all alone.

When she made the second turn on a country road he recognized, Sam's throat closed up. His chest was so tight, he couldn't breathe. But that was okay. He wasn't sure he wanted to.

He knew, before she turned, where they were going. He watched her take the curves of the cemetery road without slowing.

The car stopped suddenly, and Cassie got out, stumbling as she approached the tiny headstone. Sam was beside her without even realizing he'd gotten out of the vehicle.

He read the small stone. *Emily Carol Montford.* After Cassie's mother. And his. Emily was born five months after Sam left home. And died a month later.

Pain seared through him.

"After you left, I couldn't eat, couldn't sleep." Cassie started to talk, each word laced with a despair so deep he knew she'd never be free of it. And with each word, Sam wished he was dead, too.

"Nobody suspected I was pregnant, at first. Including me. I'd lost track of days and weeks. Upset as I was, missing a period was to be expected. But then I started getting sick to my stomach every time I ate. For a long time the doctor thought it was stress, but when it got to the point where I couldn't keep anything down, she did a pregnancy test. I was almost four months along by then. I'd had no real nutrition for two months. No rest. No vitamins…"

She was trembling, her arms wrapped around her middle. Sam wanted to haul her into his own arms and shelter her.

He was afraid to touch her.

"I tried to take better care of myself after that. Quit school, made myself stay in bed as much as possible—but that just gave me more time to think. And I still couldn't keep much food down. For a while, they had me on an I.V. at home. That seemed to help, and I gradually gained back a little of the weight I'd lost...."

Bile rose in Sam's throat. While he'd been out finding himself, his wife had been home fighting death.

Jaw clenched, he felt as though he'd been carried off in a sea of anguish so treacherous, he knew he was never going to be the same again.

"I was seven-and-a-half months along when I started to hemorrhage." She stopped, swallowed. Wiped her nose and eyes with a tissue she'd brought from the car.

She handed one to Sam. Until that moment he hadn't known he was crying.

"It all happened very quickly after that. They did a cesarean, took Emily. She was beautiful...." Her voice broke completely, and Sam had to touch her, pull her into his arms, cradle her against his heart.

"I'm so sorry," he choked. "God, Cassie, I'd rather be dead myself...."

She lifted her head, but didn't draw away. "Her lungs weren't fully developed, but they thought she had a fighting chance," Cassie told him. "She had a strong heart."

She had to stop again. Took a couple of gulps of air. "I was in bed for the first few days because of the C-section—"

"I didn't notice any scarring." Sam hung everything on that point. Surely he'd have noticed a C-section scar on Cassie's smooth belly.

"It's right in the bikini line," she told him. "They made a big deal of telling me at the time that it wouldn't show. As if I cared..."

The anguish just kept growing. His young, beautiful wife, barely beyond childhood herself, having to face such a tragedy.

Alone.

Because of him.

Turning back to the headstone, Cassie bowed her head, crying harder. But she stayed close to Sam. He didn't deserve that sweet torture. He deserved to be as utterly alone as she had been.

"By the third day, they couldn't keep me away from her," she whispered hoarsely. "I was with her every minute after that. They tried to get me to go home, but I wouldn't leave the hospital. Not once that entire month."

"How big was she?" Sam asked, remembering Mariah's birth. The squalling, kicking seven-pound bundle of health and joy that she'd been.

"Just under five pounds."

Small enough to fit in his palm. Less than a bag of sugar. A tear dripped off Sam's chin.

He stared at the headstone, as if he could some-how picture the child who'd lived for such a short time. The child he would now never see.

"Could you hold her?"

Cassie nodded. "Every day. I fed her, helped bathe her, changed the pad under her little bot-tom..."

Cassie broke down completely then, her legs go-ing limp as she fell against Sam, sobbing out ten years' worth of grief. Somehow Sam supported her weight, his gaze locked on that tiny tombstone.

Cassie was right. They couldn't ever go back.

He could never, in a million years, make this one up to her.

Or to himself.

CHAPTER SIXTEEN

CASSIE WENT ONE BETTER than getting Sam the phone number of her client, the collie breeder. Mrs. Stonethaler had had a cancellation on one of the puppies and was delighted to have Cassie bring a potential buyer out to her home. So, late Tuesday morning, after Cassie had seen to her morning appointments at the clinic, she, Sam and Mariah were in Sam's truck on their way to the Stonethaler ranch. Although the air conditioning was on full blast, it hardly seemed to help. Cassie had taken off the white lab coat she often wore at the clinic, but she still felt hot in her linen slacks and sleeveless silk blouse. Sam didn't look any more comfortable in his denim cutoffs.

Cassie couldn't tell if Mariah was comfortable or not. Her sweet face showed no sign of distress at the nearly one-hundred-degree heat. In her cute pink sundress, with its bows tied at the shoulders, she certainly *looked* cool and composed.

"Are you excited about having a puppy of your own?" Cassie asked the child. When Mariah didn't reply, Cassie continued, infusing her voice with a cheer she was trying very hard to feel. "Mrs. Stonethaler is the owner of the puppies' mommy, and she's a very nice lady. She'd be happy if you could give one of her puppies a home."

Mrs. Stonethaler raised collies, she told Mariah. Mr. Stonethaler raised Arabian horses. Cassie told Sam he ought to be glad Mariah was only in need of a puppy. An Arabian horse would have cost him thousands of dollars.

Sam nodded, brushed his free hand down Mariah's French-braided hair, and continued to drive.

Cassie fell back into the uneasy silence that had marked their relationship since they'd returned from the cemetery the other night. They'd seen each other in church the next morning, when Cassie had made a point of speaking to an unresponsive Mariah. Sam, his eyes filled with shadows, had merely nodded at her and disappeared.

Today he hadn't once met her eyes. Twice she'd started to speak to him about Emily, then stopped. He'd created such an effective wall between them, it was almost as if he wasn't there.

She should be happy about that. She was finally getting her wish—Sam Montford out of her life.

Except that she didn't feel happy.

Telling him about Emily had brought it all back. The helplessness. The fear. The anger. The guilt.

Unexpectedly, sharing it with Sam had brought her closer to him, reawakening needs, reminded her that Sam was the other half of her heart. With him she'd been able to reason out the ways of the world, make sense of them. Find a way to be peaceful with them.

But when it came to Emily's brief life, her death, there was no peace to find.

Cassie was worried about Sam. After they'd left Emily's grave, he'd shut himself off. It was the first time in her life that Cassie had been with him and completely unable to *feel* him.

It was unsettling. Frightening. As if she'd looked in the mirror and seen a face that didn't belong to her.

Mrs. Stonethaler, after showing them to the nursery, as she called it, in the sun room of her huge home, left them alone with one of the puppies that was, as yet, unclaimed. The mother and other puppies were in a large crate at the other end of the room.

"What do you think, Mariah?" Cassie asked, holding the puppy. "She looks just like Sammie, only smaller."

Mariah, clutching Sam's hand, was engrossed in the three buttons on the collar of his short-sleeved shirt.

"Has she said anything since Friday?" Cassie asked Sam. She'd wanted to ask him yesterday on the phone, when they'd made today's arrangements, but he'd had to go before she had a chance.

Glancing down at his daughter, Sam shook his head. And then said, "Mariah, don't you want to look at the puppy?" With his hands on her shoulders, he turned the child to face Cassie. "If you like her, you can have her."

Mariah stared vacantly in front of her, eyes slightly lowered.

Cassie knelt down, until the puppy was at Mariah's eye level. "You have to see if you like her, honey, before we can buy her for you. She needs to know that she's going to a home where she's wanted, or she'll be afraid."

The child blinked. Her tiny hands squeezed into fists.

Cassie tried to catch Sam's gaze, to see if he'd caught Mariah's response, but he didn't meet her eye.

"Let's sit down and see if the puppy likes us," Cassie said, pulling Mariah onto the ground with her.

Sam stood back, his expression brooding as he watched them. For a second, Cassie couldn't take her eyes off him. He looked so good to her, standing there. Fit. Sexy. Strong. His legs were defined, his stomach lean and trim at the waist, his chest straining against his polo shirt. Manual labor sure hadn't done anything to hurt Sam in the looks department.

The puppy squirmed in her arms. She'd been

gnawing on Cassie's finger—not that Cassie had even noticed.

"You're so cute!" Cassie said, raising the puppy to her face. "Look, Mariah, she has a white spot on her nose."

Mariah blinked again. Not once had she turned around to look at Sam.

Putting the puppy down, Cassie pushed the wriggling bundle over to Mariah, and then moved back. Again she tried to meet Sam's eyes. Again his focus was solely on Mariah.

With her little butt up in the air, the puppy danced around the child, smelling her hands, tasting her sandal. Then, apparently finding the child acceptable for further inspection, she climbed onto Mariah's lap. Her hands on the floor, the little girl didn't move. The puppy did enough moving for both of them. She licked Mariah's arm. Turned around several times in her lap. Jumped off. And back on.

Mariah blinked again, but sat completely still. The puppy, apparently not offended by Mariah's unresponsiveness, put her front paws on her chest, sniffing her chin. And then she lunged up, grabbing one of the ties to Mariah's dress and tugged hard.

Cassie and Sam both started forward at the same time, intending to rescue the little girl, but before either one of them could reach her, they stopped, shocked by the sound they heard.

Mariah was laughing.

She ceased abruptly, as soon as she heard herself—but it had happened. She'd taken a step forward. There was no going back now.

Cassie's gaze collided with Sam's over the child's head. His were filled with tentative hope. Gratitude. And sorrow, too.

They'd deal with that later. For now, Cassie's stomach relaxed simply because she'd connected with him again.

She'd deal with that later, too.

Motioning to Sam to stay put, Cassie left the puppy on Mariah's lap, until the puppy's exuberant attempt to untie the bows at her shoulders began to succeed and the child finally reached up with one hand to push the puppy down.

She didn't, however, push the dog away.

Cassie had an idea. "Do you want the puppy, Mariah?" she asked.

Mariah froze, as though she'd been caught doing something she shouldn't.

Moving a little closer on the ceramic-tiled floor, she lifted the little girl's chin. "If you want that puppy, she's all yours, but you have to *tell* me you do," she said seriously. "I need to know she's going to be loved, or I can't ask Mrs. Stonethaler to sell her to us."

Mariah's hand slid quickly up and down the

puppy's back. The child wanted that dog. Cassie's instincts were telling her so.

Which meant it was time to help Mariah help herself. The child had given them enough signs to let them know she was ready. Praying she wasn't pushing too hard too fast, Cassie sat back, letting go.

"I mean it, Mariah. I can't let you have that puppy unless you promise me that you really, really want her."

Sam stepped a little closer, standing protectively behind the little girl. Cassie couldn't look at him, couldn't be distracted. She had a feeling Mariah was really struggling, that she had things to tell them.

"You don't want to hurt Cassie's feelings, do you, squirt?" he asked, and Cassie breathed a little easier. He was on her side.

The child didn't say anything, but she continued to stroke the puppy's fur. And when the puppy started to squirm away, she reached out her other hand to keep her in place.

Mariah wanted that dog.

Cassie swallowed. Took a deep breath. And plunged in. "Mariah, I know you understand what we're saying to you. I know you can answer us. And I know you want that dog. What I *don't* know is why you won't talk to us. Please, sweetie. Sam and I are the only ones here. We both love you very much and we'll do anything to help, but you've got to talk to us, sweetie. You've got to tell us what's going on so we know what to do.''

When Mariah shook her head, every nerve in Cassie's body tensed. She felt Sam settle beside her, and was a little afraid to have him there.

"Why?" Cassie asked, her throat raw with the effort it took to control her emotions. "Why won't you talk to us, sweetie?"

The child's head moved slowly as she looked up at Cassie. Her eyes were clear, focused. And filled with tears. And then she lowered her head again.

"When I talked, it killed my mommy."

She'd spoken! Such beautiful sounds. Such unthinkable sentiments. Cassie felt Sam tense beside her, but didn't dare look at him. She had a job to do. Swallowing the lump in her throat, Cassie forged ahead.

"No, honey, don't ever think that," she said. "Bad men killed your mother. You had nothing to do with it."

She felt like such a fraud. She hadn't been there. Had only vague reports to go by. God only knows what images the child might be seeing as she stared at the floor.

"Are you remembering things, honey? Things you thought you'd forgotten?"

Mariah shrugged. A tear trickled off her chin.

Sam moved then, pulling his daughter onto his

lap, cradling her against him. "I know with all my heart that your mommy and daddy would want you to talk to me. You know that, don't you, Mariah?"

The little girl stared up at him, her big blue eyes filled with tears. She nodded—and then she opened that rosebud mouth and the vile stories started pouring out.

Mrs. Stonethaler, probably wondering what was taking so long, had come back to check on them, but with one look at the situation, merely whispered that they should take all the time they needed. She quietly closed the door as she left them alone.

"They had a big knife, Sam," Mariah was saying, the words once released coming so quickly that Cassie could hardly understand them. It seemed that now Mariah had decided to break her vow of silence, she couldn't get rid of her thoughts fast enough.

Cassie, stayed in the background, an outsider now. On the one hand, she could hardly believe the miracle of hearing that sweet childish voice; on the other, she was hurting with each word the child uttered. *Precious, precious little girl, you should never have seen such things.*

"They cut Daddy and made him bleed, and they hit him and made his eye all puffy and then his mouth was bleeding and he told Mommy and me how much he loved us and he told me to be brave and mind my mommy and they took him away. He couldn't walk good because they kicked his leg and he kept falling..."

Through it all, Sam's expression of warmth and love never changed. He slowly rocked the child, smoothing the hair back from her forehead. Cassie, tears streaming down her face, could only imagine what that control was costing him.

"They took some other people, too, and they went away for a while, and Mommy and me just cried and said how much we loved each other, and Mommy told me we'd see Daddy again real soon, that the men just took him out so I wouldn't see him bleeding while they got a big Band-Aid..."

Mariah's blue eyes were focused on Sam's mouth, her little finger reaching up to touch it. "I knew they weren't going to help him, Sam. They were bad men. But I didn't know about the not-breathing part. When you stop breathing, you *die*, Sam. The bad men hurt Mommy and Daddy because I talked and cried when they told me to shut up and they made them stop breathing, and I'm scared you're going to stop breathing, too...."

Her tirade ended as abruptly as it had begun. Mariah clutched Sam's shirt in her fists and buried her face against his chest.

"No, Mariah," he said soothingly. "I'm not going to stop breathing."

"I watch you, Sam. And everytime you talk, I

can't see your chest go up and down so I don't know if you're going to stop breathing...."

"And that scares you, huh?" Cassie asked, understanding so much now.

Sobbing, the little girl nodded.

Cassie reached over, rubbing Mariah's arm. "Sometimes people you care about die, honey. But then there are other people who love you who'll still be around to help you when you're lonely. They'll go on loving you and living with you and taking care of you. That's how God makes it when someone goes to live with Him."

Mariah shook her head. "Mommy wasn't there." The words were muffled against Sam's shirt.

"Wasn't where?" Sam asked, frowning.

"God's house."

Cassie could hardly make out the words, meeting Sam's look over Mariah's head. What was Mariah talking about?

"People said Mommy went to live with God, but when you took me to God's house to make Grandma happy, Mommy wasn't there."

Sam's frown cleared suddenly, and he pulled Mariah away so he could look into her eyes. "Church is called 'God's house' because that's where people go to talk to him, but He doesn't *live* there, honey. He lives up in heaven, and that's where your mommy and daddy are."

"Are...are they better now? Did they stop bleeding? They don't hurt anymore, do they?"

Sam swallowed hard.

Cassie sensed how urgently Mariah needed to know that her parents were no longer in pain. And she got her first real glimpse of the precocious child Mariah must have been before tragedy shattered her life.

"They don't hurt anymore, honey," Sam said with obvious difficulty. "They're all better. And they're looking down at you now, glad that you're better, too."

"Are you sure, Sam?" the child whispered.

"Absolutely sure."

Cassie knew there were some grueling counseling sessions ahead for the little girl, and for Sam, too. But Mariah could resume her life now.

And Cassie could finally get on with the rest of *her* life.

Whatever that was going to be.

TWO WEEKS LATER, Cassie was reading her favorite section of the Sunday morning paper—the comics—when she stopped short, chills spreading through her body.

The folks at Borough Bantam had been in a furor for weeks now, with the newcomer in their midst, and the little mouse appearing from nowhere, being adopted by the king and queen. Cassie followed her favorite comic strip religiously, had since its inception, though she couldn't explain, even to herself, what made it so special. She just knew that her week wasn't complete without it.

And now, here she was, sitting alone at her kitchen table in her pajamas on a Sunday morning, wondering, once again, where she was going to find the strength to be happy. With Mariah no longer needing her help, Cassie had only seen her and Sam twice. Once when they picked up "Teddy" from the clinic, and the second time when they brought her back in to be wormed.

Mariah was thriving. Though there were still shadows in her eyes, times when she was very quiet, she was well on the way to recovery. She was certainly thrilled to have her new puppy, and held her very tenderly. And she obviously adored Sam.

Cassie wasn't surprised. He'd be a wonderful father. She'd always known that about him.

He barely spoke to her. And never met her eyes. At first she thought it was because of her, because he was angry with her, but as soon as she'd had time to think—and talk to Phyllis—she'd figured out that it was himself he couldn't forgive.

For something he could never change.

Cassie understood that. She'd been hating him for a long time. And hating herself, as well.

And, oddly enough, this little comic strip had expressed not only the feelings she'd been struggling with, but the resolution she'd finally arrived at.

Ripping it out, Cassie hurried back to her bedroom, and quickly got dressed in a pair of shorts and a white T-shirt. She brushed her teeth and ran a comb through her hair, though she didn't take the time to pull her hair back or put it up. Then she went to find Sam before he left for church.

SAM WAS SITTING OUT FRONT in cutoff shorts, waiting for his mom and dad and Mariah to leave for church, before he headed up to his office above the garage. The only remedy he knew for what ailed him, the only way to cope with the unending regret, was to work.

He recognized Cassie's Taurus, as she pulled into his parents' drive. His heart going into overdrive, he strolled down to meet her. Something must be wrong for her to come roaring up here like that.

"We have to talk," she said, her door open before she'd even put the car in park.

"Sure," Sam said, forgetting for the moment that he'd taken himself out of her life—because the only way to lessen her pain was to stay away. Not to be a constant reminder of everything she'd lost.

She got out and shut the door. "In private."

"My office is over the garage," Sam said, leading the way. "We'll be alone there."

When they reached the office, she took a cursory

look around, seeming to approve of the big metal desk, the bookshelves covering one whole wall, the easels and tools stacked neatly in a corner. "I'm also taking over the fourth stall in the garage downstairs," he told her, "as a supply house and storeroom for the renovation business."

Cassie nodded, took a seat on the leather couch he'd brought over from his parents' attic, and slapped his comic strip down on the wood-slatted coffee table. *Borough Bantam.*

"Have you read this?" she demanded.

Things were coming at him so fast, Sam's heart was about to beat out of his chest. He hadn't seen Cassie like this since before he'd betrayed her all those years ago. So full of spunk and confidence.

What was going on?

"Yeah, I've read it," he said warily, circling the table. Did she know? Was she angry with him?

"Well, read it again," she told him. "Especially that last frame."

Sam didn't need to read it. He knew it by heart. He'd written the damn thing. But because he wasn't sure what she knew or where she was going with any of this, he picked it up and read it, anyway.

He'd written the strip shortly after Mariah's near-seizure in the gym. The king and queen had just discovered that the newcomer was the knight who'd run out on them years ago, leaving them unde-fended and defenseless when the kingdom, for the

first time in its 600-year history, came under attack.
The newcomer had returned to the Borough, to his
home, to protect its inhabitants. In his years of wandering, he'd learned much. And he'd realized that
there was nothing to be had worth having that he
couldn't find at home. The king and queen, upon
identifying him, didn't scorn him as he'd expected.
They welcomed him home, like the prodigal son.
They saw into his heart and knew that he'd never
have left them if he'd thought the Borough would
ever be at risk. He'd have given his life for them,
if he had to. At the end of the strip, the stupid
magistrate still didn't seem to realize that the newcomer was in the Borough—had no idea that his
position was being usurped. That he was going to
be replaced by someone relatively new to the Borough, a long-lost brother of the king. And he'd
managed, with carefully chosen words and pictures,
to convey all of that in one week's episode.

The ending was, as always, the magistrate in his
little circle, a worm going round and round. *I am.
I am. I am.*

"Don't you see?" Cassie said, when he looked
up. "It's us, Sam. Not *exactly,* of course, but this
is like you and me. You left, Sam, but you wouldn't
have if you'd realized how much I needed you.
You'd have given everything to be here with Emily
and me. Just like that wild kingdom would have—
to protect the kingdom."

His breath caught in his throat. Did she know? Or didn't she?

He wasn't sure what to say. Wasn't sure what *she* was saying.

"We have to forgive ourselves," Cassie said. "Both of us—we have to forgive ourselves and each other."

Sam frowned. What did she have to forgive herself for? And there couldn't possibly be anything *he* had to forgive *her* for.

"We've made some pretty serious mistakes," she said, looking up at him, her beautiful brown eyes beseeching. "I know you're hating yourself for what happened after you left town, and part of me has been hating you all these years, too. Or at least trying to."

He'd figured that out at the cemetery; hearing her give voice to the words were a knife to his heart. Cassie's hatred was the worst form of torture. But one he deserved.

"Mostly, I was so badly hurt, I couldn't do anything but try to cope with that—not to care—but when you came back, I was scared to find out that I *did* still care. And that all the hate I thought I'd stored up wasn't really there. I couldn't understand that. Until today."

She'd definitely lost him now. As her eyes reiterated what her words had just told him, his heart gave a hopeful lurch—but he knew there was no hope. Not for him. Not with her.

"What happened today?" he asked.

"I read this." She picked up the comic strip. "I wasn't just hating you, Sam. I was hating me, too. I should've known I was pregnant. I'd always been so regular, I should've suspected—"

"How could you be expected to keep track of *anything* after what I'd done to you?"

Cassie shrugged. "I should have been stronger, more…more my own person, able to handle having you gone. If I'd realized sooner, who knows what might have happened differently? Maybe if I'd taken vitamins sooner, gotten more sleep, better nutrition…"

Sam couldn't let her go on. "Cass, don't do this to yourself. You did the best you could." He sat down beside her, took both her hands in his. "Look inside yourself, honey. Listen to the truth. You know you would never have put our baby in danger, would have given your life to save her."

"I know," Cassie said, grinning through a sudden spurt of tears. "Just like in this strip," she said, waving it in front of him. "The knight would have stayed, given his life, if he'd known how badly he was needed."

Sam sat back, stunned, as he started to suspect what she was trying to say.

"You would never have left if you'd known I

was pregnant, Sam. You'd have stayed, gone to law school, become the mayor of Shelter Valley in a heartbeat, if you'd known the cost of your leaving.''

Of course he would have. But Borough Bantam was just a damn comic strip. Emily Carol Montford was his *daughter*, for God's sake.

Cassie stroked a finger across the back of his hand. ''You know, I've been doing a lot of thinking, and I can see now that I was to blame, too, long before you left town.''

''No!'' Sam said sharply. ''You were the best wife a man could ask for, Cassie. So loving. Unselfish. Doing special little things every day to let me know you loved me.''

''But I stopped listening to you with my *heart*,'' she whispered, her eyes shadowed. ''I promised to love and cherish you forever, and then, after we were married, I—I didn't hear you, Sam, because I wasn't listening. You tried to give me clues, I can see that now. That time when you asked me to look at model homes in Phoenix. You said for decorating ideas, but then you went on and on about the community center there. You were looking for a way out, and I never even gave it another thought.''

He had really liked that community center. It'd had a full-scale basketball court. An entire floor of exercise equipment. An Olympic-size swimming pool. And acres and acres of parkland.

''I should've tried harder to explain.''

"Maybe you didn't come right out and tell me what was wrong," Cassie continued. "But you didn't *know* what was wrong, so how could you make it clear to me?" Sam was moved by how much thought she'd given all of this. Moved, but not surprised. This was his Cassie—the woman he'd been loving for as long as he'd known what love was.

"You needed my help to figure things out, but I'd been too busy living the life we'd already chosen, the life people expected us to live."

"You're being very generous—you know that, don't you?" Sam asked, a wry grin on his face.

He was afraid to hope, but it felt damn good to be able to talk to her again. To really talk. With no battle-scarred walls between them.

Cassie shook her head. "I'm not, Sam," she said. "I'm being honest. With you, and with myself. I've been blaming you all these years, because without you here, it was easier to do that. But I've known, deep inside, that it was my fault, too."

Perhaps, although most of the blame was still his, he told himself. Yet she might have found a way to set him free. Because she was right. He would never have left this town if he'd thought, for one second, that tragedy would follow in his wake.

He'd left for Cassie. Because he'd been afraid, after his betrayal, after sleeping with another woman, that his staying would destroy her. He couldn't trust himself not to hurt her.

Acting purely on instinct now, Sam leaned forward, placed his lips against hers and, in the best way he knew how, begged for her forgiveness. Her lips opened to him and welcomed him home.

When the kiss turned into more, when Sam knew that if he continued he was going to have her naked on this old leather couch, he stopped. But he couldn't make himself pull away. He sat back on the sofa, pulling her close to him, instead.

If they were going to find a second chance—and he was completely determined that they were—there had to be a little more honesty. Another revelation.

"Cass? About Borough Bantam—"

"Oh, Sam, have you ever read that strip?" she interrupted.

Sam nodded, looking for the right words to tell her that he'd read every single episode that had ever been printed. Would she lose some of her faith in him if she knew he'd been using Shelter Valley all these years?

"Did it mean to you what it meant to me?" she asked him, almost eagerly.

Sam hesitated. "I don't know. What did it mean to you?"

She laughed a little self-consciously. "You're going to think I'm crazy, but I almost feel as if that strip saved my life, Sam. You have no idea how many times I was at the end of my rope, and then I'd read that thing and some simple little truth would pop out—as though it was written just for me. It always seemed to be what I needed to hear.''

His throat tight, Sam fought back the overwhelming emotion that threatened to overcome him. The true freedom she'd just given him.

He hadn't deserted her, after all.

''You do think I'm crazy,'' she said, her shoulders settling back against the couch.

''No—'' Sam started, and when his voice broke, had to start again. ''I'm thanking God there was a way for us to be together even when we were worlds apart,'' Sam said. ''If ever I needed confirmation that you and I were ordained to find each other, confirmation that what we have is stronger then either of us, this was it.''

Cassie turned, frowning as she looked at him. ''What are you talking about? The strip helped you, too?''

''I wrote that strip, Cass. I am S.N.C.''

She jumped up. ''No way!'' And sank back down, her hand on his chest as she stared at him. Then, grabbing up the comic strip, she stared at it. ''You're S.N.C. What does S.N.C. stand for?''

''Sam 'n' Cassie.''

EPILOGUE

SAM AND CASSIE MONTFORD were remarried the last weekend in May of that year. Until they found a house they just *had* to have, they were going to live with Carol and James, who weren't too proud to beg them to stay. Nor too proud to pull out all the stops, either. Mariah needed them, they said.

They sold Cassie's house to Tory and Ben, who were delighted with all the space. And the decorating. Ben was already working at Montford, Inc., and James had started to groom him for the mayoralty campaign, expecting him to take over the mayor's seat from Junior Smith in the November elections. Ben thought he was going to finish college first; Sam didn't think so.

Ben would get his college degree—Sam had no doubt of that—but he'd be reaching his other goals a lot sooner than that. Sam knew how Shelter Valley worked, and Ben would figure it out soon enough.

With a little brown bag in his hand, Sam approached the suite he was going to be sharing with

Cassie at Montford Mansion. It was his wedding night. And what a night it was going to be.

But there was something that had to be done first.

"Sam?" Cassie called from the open bathroom door. He heard the sound of water, telling him she was in the double-wide garden tub.

"Yeah?" he asked. He shouldn't be feeling relieved by the brief reprieve her bath was giving him. But he was. A little weak in the knees, he sat down on the side of the bed.

He was probably wrong. Putting himself through this for nothing. Would be putting *her* through it in a couple of minutes, too. But if there was one thing Sam did well, it was to learn from his mistakes.

"Can I ask you something?" she called out.

"Sure." Dropping the bag on his dresser as he passed, Sam stood in the bathroom doorway. And almost talked himself out of the test he was planning. Cassie looked stunning, lounging back against the side of the tub, bubbles caressing her milky skin, her breasts and nipples provocatively revealed.

"Why did every episode end with *I am, I am, I am?*"

So far, Borough Bantam was still his and Cassie's secret, but she was nagging him to share it. She was sure everyone in Shelter Valley would be proud as hell. He figured, eventually, that she was going to win this one.

"I wondered that for a long time myself," Sam admitted now, thinking about her question. "He was a worm, something most people think of as slimy and disgusting."

"Which is how you saw yourself."

"Maybe."

She arched her brow at him.

"Okay, yes. But he also represented the never-changing values of Shelter Valley. It took me a while to figure all this out. Regardless of what happens in the world, we can always count on the people here to continue, to be who they are. Family and community are the things that matter to us. It's been that way for over a hundred years.

"It was how I reminded myself that Shelter Valley, and my place here—whatever that turned out to be—were waiting."

Cassie smiled at him. "I thought you'd say you were trying to send me a message."

Sam shrugged, a little embarrassed. "I think I was. I just didn't dare hope you'd ever get that message."

Cassie's eyes brimmed with tears. "I got it, Sam. How could I not? It was from you."

Sam turned, reaching for the bag on the other side of the doorway. If he didn't do this now, it wouldn't get done.

"Hey, mister." She called him back. "You wanna join me?"

Taking a deep breath, Sam turned again. "I want you to get out, Cass," he said. "At least for a minute."

Frowning, probably at his tone of voice, Cassie sat up, holding a washcloth over her breasts. "What's wrong?" And then she saw the bag. "What's in there?"

Sam pulled out the box he'd bought earlier that day, when he'd gone into town to pick up Cassie's flowers for the simple ceremony they'd had in the living room at Montford Mansion.

"No," Cassie said as soon as she saw the box.

"Yes."

"Don't do this, Sam." Her eyes were full of tears. "We're so lucky to have Mariah. And we can adopt others if we want to. But don't keep hoping. I can't bear to hope with you—"

Her voice broke, and she stood, reached for a towel, began drying herself.

"You haven't had a period in almost two months, Cassie."

He'd asked again the day she'd come to his office, and she'd told him she hadn't had one yet but had assured him she would soon. They'd been making love ever since, and Sam knew for a fact that it hadn't happened yet.

"I've been irregular ever since Emily." She said the words softly but firmly. She wanted no part of this.

But he wasn't giving up. "Please, Cass, just humor me here? It's not even that I'm hoping, because I'm not. I've got you, and that's enough to keep me happy for twenty lifetimes." He turned her to face him, his eyes earnest as he looked into hers. "You had problems before because you didn't find out you were pregnant in time. Every day that your period isn't here, I'm more afraid of what might be happening, what could go wrong. Please, won't you take a couple of minutes to set my mind at ease?"

Cassie held his gaze for another couple of minutes, then grabbed the box from him. "Give me a little privacy, will you?" she grumbled.

His wife was not happy with him.

Sam left the room, but didn't close the door. He didn't want her feeling trapped in there, all alone.

As soon as he could tell she was finished, he went back in.

"How about we get back in that tub now?" he asked.

"Don't you want to wait for the results? It'll only be a minute."

Sam shook his head. He'd check later, just to make sure she was right. And then the worry would be behind him.

Dropping her towel, Cassie climbed back into the tub, but she was distracted. Sam undressed and joined her. She didn't even seem to notice he was there.

She finally just got out. Dripping water all over the bathroom, she headed for the little vial with the stick. "Damn it, why did you have to do this?" she cried. "I was just fine until you—"

Her voice stopped, and the stick in her hand fell to the floor.

"What?" Sam asked, flooding the floor as he leaped out of the tub.

Cassie looked up at him, tears streaming down her face, a joy that he'd never seen before in her luminous brown eyes. A spiritual joy, a connection, that he felt clear to the depths of his heart.

"I am," she said. *"I am. I am."*